BOOK 1

HANNAH STENFORS

The Night The Moon Trembled — Book 1

Printed in the United States of America

ISBN-13: xxx-x-xxxx-xxx

CONTENTS

Prologue

They say that when you feel the end is near, you start to have flashbacks of the beginning. As I stood with tears unconsciously running down my face and blood splattered all over my body, I couldn't help but turn to him. As he ran toward me, his hair stuck to his face and his eyes flaring blue with determination, he shouted at me to run. His face filled with passion and anger, and his aura screamed with protection.

Everything in my head slowed down. I couldn't have moved even if I'd wanted to. The more I stood in place, the angrier he became. He knew that if I stayed, I would die. But the truth was, I wouldn't want to die anywhere else but here, by his side. Forgetting the world, the pain, the lies, and the cards I'd been dealt, I smiled at him.

He roared in anger. He knew I wasn't leaving. He knew I was preparing for my death. The face of evil began to walk toward me, dragging the blood-stained sword on the ground. It all came flooding back to me, how I'd gotten to this moment, how I'd fallen in love with the man running toward me, how a would-be college student had come to stand face to face with the evilest being on Earth. My mind started drifting back to the beginning.

CHAPTER 1

THE BEGINNING

Water. Such sweet bliss yet such deep sorrow. Ask the man who traveled for two days without water how sweet and blissful water is. Ask the man whose family drowned in a horrifying typhoon how water brought him such sadness. Everyone has different opinions for different reasons.

My neighbor Catherine hated the ocean. She was deathly afraid of stingrays, sharks, and any other sea creature at that. But I loved it. Not for the iconic scenery or the people. Not even for the famous Florida sunshine. My favorite part was the silence. When I let the ocean pull me into its depths of pure and blissful silence, I could really connect with myself. I heard nothing; I felt nothing; I was nothing but a weightless particle floating under the waves. Away from the noise, away from the pain, away from everything.

"Hey, I don't pay you to swim all day. Get a bucket and keep it moving," said my overbearing boss. She thought everybody owed her something.

"Hey, Rose!" Tyler came paddling over. With his long, lanky body, it didn't take him long to reach his destination.

"Hey, Ty," I said with a halfhearted smile. I knew what was coming.

"So," Tyler said without missing a beat. "How have you been? Wait. Better yet, where have you been hiding these past couple days?" he asked, shaking his long blond dreadlocks like a dog that had been sprayed with the hose.

I inwardly smiled, thinking about how I could see Tyler as a dog; he was energetic, playful, and I swore he could hear a pin drop from a mile away. "I've been well," I told him. "And you know me. I'm always doing homework or working here. No changes in my exciting world."

He sighed. "Yeah, I know, but ever since the banshee moved me to the other side of the aquarium with the whales, I never get to see you anymore."

I chuckled at Tyler's description of our boss. Tyler had never liked Mrs. Bernard, but I could see how her loud, scratchy German voice could be compared to the screeching cries of a banshee.

He smiled as well, knowing exactly what I was laughing at.

Tyler knew me so well; he'd been my best friend since we were children. It was going to be sad when I left him behind to go to Colorado, but it had been a long seventeen years here in Jacksonville, Florida, and it was time to move forward. My eighteenth birthday was just one day away, and so was my high school graduation.

"You know, graduation's tomorrow, and Toby's throwing a big party on the beach," Tyler said, redirecting my thoughts away from Colorado and my birthday.

"I know," I said unenthusiastically. I wasn't big on going to huge social events. I was much more of a thinker than a talker. "I don't think I'll make it. I have to keep working on my jeep. I'm almost finished," I said, my voice growing high-pitched. I lied terribly. The jeep had months of work left on it.

Tyler always knew when I lied. I never looked him in the eye, and he said my voice got higher and squeakier. He gave me a disapproving look, rolling his eyes. "I don't know why you don't just let that hunk of rust go. It hasn't worked in months."

The truth was it would take a miracle for old Betsy to start up again. But that jeep was part of the last memory I had with my mom before she'd passed last year. I remembered her passing like it had been yesterday.

We'd been driving to the beach for our usual monthly stroll, where she told me all her inner thoughts and asked me to tell her mine. My mother and I had such a strong connection. Don't get me wrong, I loved my dad, but my mom had really understood me.

As we'd been about to get out of the car, I'd seen a bright light, and within a split second, terror had struck my mother's face. White light as fast as lightning had blinded me. After that, I just remembered screams of pain. I didn't know if they'd been my screams or my mother's, but they were so loud, like sirens, that I knew I'd never forget the sound.

I'd woken up in the ER, feeling like I was waking up from a nightmare. Pain had struck my left arm as soon as I'd opened my eyes, and my head had been pounding. I hadn't known where I was or what had happened. A nurse had heard me screaming and rushed to put more medicine in my IV to ease the pain. As I'd felt the cold anesthetic pump slowly through my veins, like a cold snake slithering through my body, I'd looked at her, and it had all come back to me. Like someone had shot the memory into my head.

I'd bombarded the nurse with questions. "Where is my mother? What happened? Can I leave? Is my mom okay?"

She'd just shushed me, telling me that I had a bad concussion and needed to rest. But I couldn't rest, not even for a second. I'd finally gotten her to tell me after five minutes of pleading.

She'd told me that a truck driver had fallen asleep at the wheel. She'd paused, looking at me as if I were a starving child on the street. There had been such pity in her eyes. "Your mother didn't make it, sweetheart," she'd said.

My heart had felt like someone had ripped it out of my chest. I'd screamed and cried hysterically. I'd ripped the IV out of my arm and started running to the desk. It had taken my dad and three doctors to get me back to my bed. Because a driver had fallen asleep at the wheel, my mother had paid the price with her life.

I shook my head, trying to shake away the memories of that day. Tyler stepped out of the water, his jet-black wetsuit clinging to his flawless surfer-boy body. As I analyzed Tyler, I wondered to myself why I'd never let it get too far between us. Tyler had made blatant comments about us going out, but I'd always turned it back into just being friends. I just didn't feel that way about him, even though a lot of girls at school did. Tyler was the captain of the swim team, and he was beyond brilliant. He passed all his classes with ease and even helped tutor others. He was a true catch. I just wasn't the right net.

He looked at me impatiently. "Are you coming?" he asked.

I let the water wash over me one last time before I leaped out and returned to the real world.

I woke up gasping like a fish out of water. I kept breathing in, but nothing was happening. Finally, after ten seconds, I began to feel air rushing into my lungs. I swallowed it hungrily, like a baby taking its first breath. I slowly wiped the long black strands of hair that were stuck to my forehead by sweat. It was the fourth time this month I'd woken up like this. I needed to relax more.

I rolled over and looked at the time on my alarm clock. 3 a.m. I had to be up in three hours. I groaned and turned back over. I tossed and turned for about two more hours before I finally dozed off, but my reprieve didn't last long.

Beep, beep, beep. I reached for the snooze button, but instead of the glorious sound of silence, I got the loud crash of my alarm clock falling to the floor. The sound jerked me right out of bed. I sat on the edge of my mattress, trying to build up enough strength to move. Then I dragged myself to the bathroom to take a long, peaceful shower.

After fifteen minutes, my dad did his usual quarter-hour check, reminding me that I didn't want to be late. What he really meant was that he didn't want the water bill to be any higher than it had been last month.

"Out in a minute!" I yelled back to him. My usual response, which really meant that I'd be at least ten more minutes.

I finished my steaming hot shower and stepped out, looking at the foggy mirror in front of me. I wiped just enough mist off that I could see my face. Looking at my reflection, I could see my mother. Her long jet-black hair had been the same length as mine. My eyes were lighter green, but they had the same hint of hunter green in them as hers had had. My skin was more olive-toned than hers had been; my mother had always been fair, probably because she'd done most of her research in Colorado. I was a tiny bit shorter than her, but overall, I was her spitting image.

My mother had been an archeologist and a very good one too. People from all over the world had used to call her to help them on archeological digs. She'd rarely come up empty-handed. She'd worked so much that she'd barely had time for her family. My parents had gotten a divorce right before my thirteenth birthday. Even though she'd worked so much, my mom had always tried to make it for our Sunday strolls once a month. That was what had made them so special.

"Rose, what are you doing up there? Are you okay?" my dad yelled from downstairs.

I chuckled. What did he think would happen to me in the bathroom? He'd been more worried about me since my mother's passing, even in the simplest of situations. "Yes, I'm fine," I called back.

He grumbled. "You should hurry up. Graduation's in forty-five minutes."

I rushed out of the bathroom and grabbed my favorite pair of jeans and my purple cotton t-shirt. I put on my jeans and my bra and started brushing the knots out of my hair.

I heard a faint clicking sound coming from the window that stopped me in my tracks. It didn't do it again, so I continued to brush my hair. I walked to the dresser and took my shirt off the hanger. Then I heard the clicking sound again. This time, it turned into a loud bang.

I grabbed the closest thing to me, a can of hairspray, and ran over to the window. I pulled back the curtain as fast as I could, and someone jumped into the room, crashing me and him to the floor.

I sprayed the hairspray, aiming for the eyes of the intruder, but instead of hearing cries of pain, I heard hysterical laughter.

When the mist from the hairspray cleared, I saw Tyler in his black and purple cap and gown. He had his blond dreads pulled back in a ponytail, and he'd shaved the little goatee he usually had hanging under his chin. He looked handsome, very clean-cut and dapper, not like his usual laid-back self. He was trying hard to hold his composure and talk without laughing.

I fought to keep my heart from jumping out of my chest. I should have known. Tyler used to bother me when we were kids, sneaking through my window at night. Sometimes, it was to scare me. Other times, we would play games and talk about the things going on in our lives. My dad caught him one time and gave him a good wringing out. Looking at him now, I couldn't help thinking he might have deserved it.

Tyler finally stopped laughing and stuttered out, "What were you going to do with the can of hairspray? Out of everything you could have grabbed in this room, you grab hairspray." He grinned.

I gave him a sideways glance, my eyes narrowing. He was right, though. I didn't know what I'd been thinking. Hairspray really wasn't going to do much to anybody.

Then Tyler's whole demeanor changed in the blink of an eye. The wide joker smile fell from his face and turned into a soft, gentle one. His light blue eyes, just a moment ago filled with tears of laughter, turned a soft and vibrant blue, a hint of lust visible in them.

I looked down to see what he was looking at. I'd been so startled by his intrusion that I'd forgotten I was only wearing my bra and jeans. I blushed and immediately turned around to put my T-shirt on.

Tyler's eyes remained on me the whole time.

I always felt uncomfortable when he got that look in his eyes. I wanted to lighten the mood. "So, you ready for new beginnings?" I asked as I grabbed my cap and gown.

Tyler smiled his infamous heartbreaker smile. "I'm always ready for new beginnings." He pulled a little black box out of his pant pocket. "I got you a little something for your birthday."

I scowled at him. "I said no gifts."

He gave me the look I could never stay mad at. "It's nothing big, I promise. I just wanted you to have something to remember me by when you go to Colorado."

I sighed in the defeat, took the box, and opened it. Inside was a unique black rope necklace with a turquoise stone in the middle. I loved it. It reminded me of the ocean. I smiled and gave him a hug. "Thank you," I said. "Now, let's not be late for our graduation."

As Tyler climbed back out the window, I gave him a slight push, which caused him to stumble a bit. We both laughed. I closed the window and put on my necklace. It was time for my new life to begin.

Tyler Chapman stood up, and the whole swim team hooted.

I clapped and smiled as I watched my friend walk proudly across the stage. *Okay, I'm coming up*, I thought nervously. I started biting my nails. I hated the fact that I had to walk across the stage in front of hundreds of people. I prayed that I wouldn't fall.

"Ronald Charman," the principal called with a smile on her face.

I was coming up next. I began to stand up.

"Darrel Danker," said the principal.

Cheers exploded throughout the auditorium.

I looked up and saw that Tyler had the same confused look written across his face. I looked down and realized that I was still standing; people were beginning to stare. I sank back down in my seat, confused, frustrated, and wanting nothing more than to disappear. In my mind, I ran over every possible explanation, but I still couldn't understand why my name hadn't been called. *Rose Chassidy*, I thought to myself. It should have been right after Ronald Charman.

I sat through the whole graduation, hoping my name would come up somewhere along the line, reshuffled into the wrong place in the alphabet. It had to have been a mistake. Maybe it had been printed in the wrong column.

Eventually, the last name, Elijah Zachary, was called. By then, I had no nails left to bite, and I had no hope either. I was devastated. As everybody separated to greet their families, I sat in my chair, feeling like I was in a twilight zone.

Tyler ran up to me as soon as he could get away from his family. He bent down and rested his hands on my knees. "What the hell's going on? I know you finished all your credits. Why didn't they call your name?"

I heard his words, but my mind was going a million miles a minute, and I couldn't answer. I blinked hard, looking past him. Finally, I was able to splutter out, "I don't know."

Tyler smiled kindly. "Well, don't you worry. We're going to handle this mess tomorrow morning," he promised. "Don't let this ruin your birthday."

Tyler was such a good friend. Something about his presence and his ever-calm demeanor reassured me that if anybody could help me, it was him. He was definitely what people called a teacher's pet. He knew most of the administrators and teachers personally, and he was liked by them all.

I took in a deep breath, met eyes with him, and sighed. "Tomorrow," I agreed. We could deal with it tomorrow.

My dad came over, looking as confused and frustrated as I felt. "Honey, are you okay?" he asked me. "I saw you stand up. Why didn't they call your name?" He planted a hand on my shoulder.

"I have no idea," I told him. "Tyler and I are going to get more information tomorrow."

My dad was not a very nosy man. He knew a girl needed her space. He didn't press me for any more answers. Instead, he kissed me on the forehead and said, "No matter what, sweetheart, I will always be proud of you."

I smiled back at him. Somehow, those words made all the difference. I wandered outside aimlessly, ready to head home.

"Rose, let me give you a ride," Tyler said, rolling up in his black BMW, concern still rising in his voice.

I was in no mood to disagree.

When I returned home, I was mentally and emotionally exhausted. I went to the garage to get an iced tea out of the freezer. But something in the garage wasn't quite right. "No!" I stopped mid-stride. My mother's jeep, my jeep, was gone. All that was left were the oil stains on the gray floor. My heart began to race, and my head spun as I tried to think of what could have happened.

"Dad!" I yelled. I bolted out of the garage into the backyard, but before I could say anything more, my dad interrupted me.

"Surprise!" he said. He wore a wide grin and stood in front of a freshly painted hunter-green Jeep Cherokee, fully rejuvenated. He looked proud of himself.

I couldn't hold back the tears, some of them from frustration, some of joy. I ran to my dad and hugged him like I never had before.

"Ahh, it's no biggie," he said sheepishly. But it was a big deal. It was the biggest thing he had ever done for me. My dad was no rich man, and he must have had to save up a lot for this.

I stepped back and took a good look at it. It looked just like it had two years ago, before the accident. My heart filled with joy, and I smiled brightly.

"Well," my dad huffed, "aren't you going to take her for a spin?" He handed me the keys.

I put the keys in the ignition, and the jeep roared to life. I knew it was crazy how something as seemingly insignificant as an old jeep could bring me so much happiness, but it gave me the inspiration I needed. I was going to get back on track. I was going to achieve my dream of going to college in Colorado, of going to the same college my mother had attended. I was going to set my sights firmly on becoming the second-best archeologist the world had ever known.

CHAPTER 2

ROAD TRIP

"Mrs. Matthews," Tyler said with the kind of smile teachers always lapped up. "I'm very close to Rose. I helped her throughout her senior year. I know she passed all of her classes."

Mrs. Mathews pursed her lips and looked down at me—no mean feat in her five-inch heels. She sized me up, poising to give me my verdict. She then redirected her gaze to look back at Tyler. "Well, Mr. Chapman, that's all very well, but Miss Chassidy's transcript says otherwise. It says she failed her math class by three points."

Undeterred, Tyler kept his voice smooth and persuasive. "I understand that, but it has to be a mistake. Do you mind if we take a look at the original transcripts?"

Mrs. Matthews's face turned stone cold. She could have passed for an ice queen with her slicked-back blond hair and icy blue eyes. She gave me a look of disapproval. "We do not make errors, Mr. Chapman. Now, if you could please excuse yourself from my office, I have real work to attend to."

Tyler was taken aback; I could read it all over his face. We left the office even more confused.

Tyler didn't have much to say on the way back to my house. He was lost in thought. He wasn't used to administrators talking down to him and refusing to give him what he wanted. Sometimes, a nice smile and a good-looking face weren't enough.

When we pulled up to my house, Tyler turned his head to say something, but before he could, something caught his eye, and a smile spread across his lips. "I don't believe it," he said, opening his door.

I smiled smugly, knowing exactly what he was talking about: my freshly painted jeep.

"You finished it," he said, coming over to my side to open my door for me.

"No," I said regretfully. I wished I could have said yes, just to rub it in. "My dad finished it for my birthday."

"Wow," he said. He walked around my new jeep, nodding in appreciation.

"Good thing I didn't listen to you and take it to the junkyard," I said, still feeling smug.

"Hey, it still doesn't beat a BMW." Tyler cocked his head.

I grinned proudly. "I'll take this jeep over your BMW any day. It has character."

"Like you," Tyler said. He bumped his shoulder into mine and let it linger there just a little too long.

I laughed and pushed him back.

When my dad and I sat down for dinner that evening, I explained everything to him, how Mrs. Matthews had said I'd failed my math class by three points, even though I knew for a fact that I'd passed it.

"You've worked a lot these past three months. Are you sure you didn't miss too many classes?" he asked me.

I cleared my throat. "Dad, I know you were working a lot. You trusted me to be responsible for my schedule, and I promise you I didn't miss any classes."

My dad nodded, looking confused. "Well, I'll talk to the school board tomorrow and see what I can do."

I smiled at his nice gesture, but I had a feeling he was going to get the same response I had. Nevertheless, I wasn't worried. I was going to get to the bottom of this.

It was about 6:30 p.m. when I decided to call it a night and head to bed. Before I could climb under the covers, the phone rang. I picked it up. "Hello?"

"Hello, is this Rose Chassidy?" said the voice on the other end of the line.

"Yes, this is her."

"This is Mrs. Wale, the vice principal. It seems there was a mistake in your transcript. We are deeply sorry. If you would like to come and pick up your diploma tomorrow morning, we would be more than happy to give it to you."

I almost dropped the phone.

"Hello? Miss Chassidy?" Mrs. Wale asked.

"Yes, I'm here," I replied. "I'll be there in the morning. Thank you." I hung up the phone, and relief washed over me. I called Tyler right away to tell him the good news.

The next morning, Tyler came with me to pick up my diploma. I'd been hoping Mrs. Matthews would be the one to hand it to me—that would show her—but when I walked in, I saw Mrs. Wale. "Miss Chassidy, darling! How are you, dear?" She didn't pause to wait for a response. "Again, I apologize for the inconvenience, but mistakes do happen." She smiled warmly as she handed me my diploma.

"I understand," I said. "I'm just relieved that you found the problem and fixed it." I paused for a moment. "What exactly was the problem?"

Mrs. Wale sighed as if irritated that I'd asked. "It seems that somehow, the teacher's grade was entered wrong.

It must have been a computer malfunction. This has never happened before, but I'm glad Mr. Chapman brought it to our attention."

I shook my head, looking over at Tyler, who smiled. I rolled my eyes. I wasn't satisfied with that answer, but I had my diploma, and that was all that mattered, so I left without questioning it any further.

The next two weeks went quickly. I was busy packing and figuring out my schedule for college. Finally, the day came for me to leave, setting off for Bluntin College in beautiful Colorado. As I hugged my dad goodbye, he reminded me of my deal. "Don't forget to call every week and visit on breaks." He was sniffling, but he coughed in a vain attempt to cover it up.

"I'm going to miss you too, Dad."

He rubbed the top of my head, then let go.

I took one last look at my house. The big oak tree in the front where I'd built my first treehouse, the off-yellow paint that made it look kind of sickly, and the brown grass that never seemed to want to go green. I would miss it all, but I knew I was doing the right thing. I'd already said goodbye to Tyler, which had been heart-wrenching, but he had promised he would visit me in a month, so at least I had something to look forward to.

As I sat in my jeep, my head spun, and the world seemed to spin with it. I grabbed the wheel to help balance myself. After a minute or two, I felt normal again. I probably hadn't eaten enough; when I got busy, I sometimes forgot to eat. I decided to go to the grocery store and pick up a couple of snacks for the road. It was going to be a long drive.

I decided to stop in Kansas to spend the night; it was only eight hours away from Colorado and seemed like a nice quiet place to rest. Driving took forever, but at last, the Kansas sign came into view. "Finally," I said out loud. By then, my butt was numb, and my eyes felt ready to close of their own accord from lack of sleep. I pulled into the Eight Balls Motel, eyeing the glowing sign. Half the letters didn't light up, so it spelled 'ight all.' The place was so vacant that it almost looked closed. I hoped desperately that it was open.

I walked toward the front doors, and they creaked open, but still, there was no sign of anybody around. I took a short stroll through the lobby, looking at the pictures on the walls. Some were eye-catching, paintings of vibrant flowers and beautiful scenes that contrasted with the dirty brown walls and floors. But some of the pictures showed black trees and mosaic oceans. *Odd-looking paintings*, I thought. I started to look for the artist's name but was soon interrupted by the appearance of an older woman, who startled me out of my reverie.

"Can I help you, dearie?"

I jumped a little, breaking my concentration. I coughed lightly, trying to hide my surprise. "Yes, I'd like a room, please."

She looked me up and down. "Just you?" she asked, raising a judgmental eyebrow.

"Yes, just me," I told her, feeling a little defensive.

"Why, you're awfully pretty to be spending the night alone here," the woman said. She flashed me a smile, revealing two teeth missing from the top row. "Most girls who come through these parts don't come alone."

For some reason, I felt a chill creep up my spine. I didn't know what she was trying to insinuate, but I didn't want to find out. "Just me," I repeated, trying to sound unaffected by her questions and unsettling demeanor. "One room will be fine."

The woman shrugged. "Very well. We don't accept credit cards, and cash is due upfront. Thirty dollars a night and free coffee and bagels at 8 a.m."

I nodded and pulled the money out of my pocket. She gave me the key, and I headed up to my room, where surprisingly, I had what might have been the best sleep of my life.

I woke to the sun softly caressing my face. *What a nice way to wake up*, I thought. I turned my head toward the alarm clock to see what the time was. 9:45 a.m. What?

There was no way I'd slept that long! I jumped out of bed, throwing on a pair of jeans and a long-sleeve shirt. I wondered if I could still make it for the free coffee. I grabbed my car keys and rushed out the door. Bam! I crashed right into a tall man with honey-brown eyes.

I stumbled back a few feet, then balanced myself. I shook my head and was about to apologize when the man started talking.

"You should watch where you're going," he spat out in a deep, penetrating voice, anger laced in his tone. He brushed off his black jacket as if I'd gotten him dirty.

Before he could say another word, I brushed past him and gave him a wicked side glance. I had no time to argue with an entitled and infuriating man, not even a handsome one. And he was handsome, all right. Dark-brown hair to his shoulders, honey-brown eyes, and a face that was sculpted to pure perfection. My heart fluttered. I snapped back my thoughts, mentally scolding myself. I redirected to anger. Who was he to speak to me like that? Like I'd done something horrific. It was an accident.

I sighed and rushed to the front desk, still agitated by the encounter with the handsome man. I then heard a loud beep from the side window, and I turned my head. Through the window, I saw a tow truck hauling away a green Jeep Cherokee. This could not be happening.

I ran as fast as my short legs would let me go. I reached the driver's side of the tow truck, hitting the window with a little too much force.

A sweaty, overweight middle-aged man with a receding hairline rolled down his window. "What do you want, lady?"

I squinted my eyes in agitation. "Well, for starters, my car back," I huffed, trying to catch my breath.

He looked me up and down and put the toothpick in his mouth. "For three hundred dollars cash, you can have the car back."

I sighed in exasperation. I only had one hundred until next week.

He continued talking. "This vehicle was parked in a handicapped spot, young lady. It's a five-hundred-dollar fine, easy. Plus, you would have to pick it up at the compound. I'm cutting you a deal. Three hundred cash now, and it's yours."

I looked around, mind racing with frenzied thoughts of what to do. "Can you give me an hour?" I pleaded.

He looked me up and down again and grunted in reluctant agreement. "Unless there's something else you're going to offer." His tone made my stomach turn.

I glared at him sharply, and he got the hint.

"Your loss." He shrugged. "You've got until 1 p.m." He wrote down his number on the back of a business card, which he handed me with a wink.

I called my dad three times, but there was no answer. He must have been out fishing; it was a Monday. I started feeling nauseous. I called Tyler—no answer. "What kind of bad luck do I have?" I asked myself.

With forty-five minutes left, I decided to go get some coffee to calm my nerves. I collected my things and checked out of the hotel. As I walked toward the lobby, I ran into the woman I'd encountered the night before.

"Hello, dearie. Did you sleep well?" she asked, grinning her toothless grin.

I smiled nervously back at her. "Yes, it was quite relaxing. Thank you. I love how quiet it was. I couldn't hear a sound from outside."

She nodded. "Yes, all these rooms are soundproof. You couldn't hear a baby screaming through those doors."

Somehow, that didn't make me feel good. "So, is the coffee still available?" I asked, feeling increasingly in need of a pick-me-up.

The woman nodded. "Take as much as you need. It's right through those double doors to your right."

I didn't waste another second. I walked quickly to the doors and opened them to find a half-pot of cold coffee sitting on the table next to a plate of stale bagels. I wasn't picky. I poured myself a cup and took a sip. The bitterness hit my taste buds, and I scrunched up my face in disapproval. I heard a low chuckle behind me and turned my head to see a red-haired guy who looked to be in his early twenties. He was tall, maybe six foot four, and he was very broad-shouldered, built like a football player. He was unconventionally attractive.

The man began to speak. "You know there's a microwave right behind the wall." He pointed to my left.

I scoffed. "I'm aware," I said in a high-pitched voice, a dead giveaway that I was lying. "I like my coffee cold." I took another bitter sip, fighting to keep my distaste from showing.

He smiled even wider. "I'm sure," he said disbelievingly. "Where are you from?" He strolled over gracefully.

"Florida," I replied. "And you?"

He smiled deeply, revealing dimples in each of his cheeks. "I'm from Kentucky," he said in a country accent.

I chuckled.

"What brings you this way?" The man poured himself some coffee and put it in the microwave.

I took my last sip of cold, bitter coffee before answering. "I need to get on the road somehow," I told him. "My first day of school is tomorrow. I'm going to Bluntin College in Colorado. I stopped here on the way." I started walking to the door. I'd surprised myself by being so open with this stranger. It wasn't like me at all.

The man nodded. "Well, it was nice meeting you …" He stopped midsentence. "I'm sorry. What was your name?"

I looked back for a split-second. "Rose," I said, opening the door.

He gave me a smirk. "Beautiful name. Very fitting. Mine is Lou. It was nice to meet you, Rose. Hopefully, I'll be seeing you around campus."

I stopped walking abruptly. "You're going to Bluntin College?" I asked, surprised.

He laughed. "I've been going there. This is my senior year." He sat back and let his eyes rake over me as if examining every part of me. "I take it this is your first year?"

I nodded.

He kept his eyes on me in a way that made me feel as though he could read my every thought. "I'm actually about to head there now," he said as he began getting up.

My mind raced. He'd been there for years. Surely, he knew how to get there. Maybe there was a bus I could take if I couldn't get my jeep back in time.

"That's nice. Do you know your way around here pretty well?" I asked.

"I would say so." He stepped closer to me. "Why? Do you need some help?" He raised one eyebrow.

Before I could answer, in walked the rude and handsome man I'd run into earlier.

My anger came flooding back. I didn't even realize I was glaring at him until Lou snapped me out of it.

"Rose?"

I shook my head.

"Are you good?" he asked, studying my face.

"Oh, yeah, sorry. I just got distracted," I said, brushing myself off.

His expression was unreadable. "Do you know that man who just walked in?" He glared at the man with a look on his face I couldn't interpret.

"No," I huffed. "I just had a brief encounter with him this morning, and I don't want to have another."

He laughed. "That bad, huh?"

I smiled.

"So," Lou continued. "It sounded like you were about to ask me something?"

"I was going to ask if you knew if there were any bus stations around here," I said.

Lou laughed hysterically. "Bus stations! You do know you're in Kansas, right?"

I sighed. "I'm taking that laugh as confirmation that there are no bus stations, then?"

"Well, I guess girls from Florida aren't as dull as I thought," Lou said.

I smiled. "You shouldn't always believe what you hear."

"Why do you want to know if there's a bus?" Lou asked. "If you need a ride to school, I'd be happy to take you myself. I'm always happy to help a damsel in distress."

At that moment, my phone rang. I took it out of my back pocket. Tyler's name flashed across the display. "Oh, thank God," I said out loud. I asked Lou to excuse me.

I told Tyler everything that had happened and asked him if he would run over to my dad's and ask if I could borrow the money I needed.

"Okay," Tyler said hesitantly. He seemed concerned. I reassured him that I was fine.

"Do you need me to come up there?" Tyler asked.

"Tyler, I'm good," I said. "It's just a small obstacle. Please just get my dad to call me as soon as possible, okay?"

"Rose, just be careful," Tyler warned me. "There are a lot of stories about girls getting taken and sold into sex-trafficking. Don't be too friendly to people."

I laughed. "Oh, yes. You should be worried. I'm Mrs. Outgoing."

Tyler laughed lightly. "Okay, you're right. Maybe I'm just missing my best friend. I have no one to share my pain at work now. You'll be home for Christmas break, right? You promised."

I said I would be.

After about five more minutes of laughing with Tyler, he said he would go over to my dad's or to the fishing grounds, where my dad usually was. I hung up the phone and started to head back toward the coffee room, only to see the rude guy sitting there, looking sullen and drinking coffee. I took a deep breath and strode past him.

As I returned to talk to Lou, I saw the man in my peripheral vision. He was staring at me and smirking. *What a pompous jerk*, I thought.

Suddenly, he dropped his coffee cup. I turned toward him and saw that he had a hand pressed to his lips, and his jaw was clenched tightly. I walked toward him, all anger leaving my mind, replaced by compassion. Ever since my mother had died and I'd felt the unfathomable pain of losing a part of myself, I'd had a strong sense of compassion for others in pain.

"Are you okay?" I asked him.

He didn't answer. He continued to clutch his mouth, bent double on the chair.

I walked even closer, not stopping until my face was inches from his. "Are you all right?" I asked, growing more and more concerned.

To my surprise, he started laughing.

Confusion made me reel back.

"You're asking if I'm okay?" He cackled hysterically, letting go of his jaw and looking up in disbelief. Then he looked at me seriously. "Are you okay?" he asked in a condescending tone. His eyes sparkled with amusement.

I straightened my back and stood up, looking down at him with my hands on my hips. "Oh, I'm fine,"

I told him coldly. "I'm not the one looking like a pansy, clutching my mouth because my coffee was a wee bit too hot." I turned quickly, stumbling a bit, and walked out. I was done talking for today. I sat outside in the parking lot, fighting to remind myself why I wasn't turning around and going to college in Florida instead.

After ten minutes, my father called me and said he would transfer the money into my bank. "Rose, you know you can always come back home," he told me.

I felt the pain of disappointment. It had only been a day, and I was already asking for help. "I know that," I said gently. "It was my fault, but trust me, I will pay you back every penny." Guilt riddled me. I knew my father was barely making ends meet. We'd been struggling since the costs of my mother's funeral. You'd think being a well-known archeologist would pay more, but sadly, it was a job people did for the love of it, for history and the truth.

"Oh, honey, stop it," my dad said as if knowing what I was thinking. "I'm fine. You just make sure to call me when you make it to your dorm."

Still feeling guilty, I whispered, "I will, Dad."

I hung up and called the tow truck driver. When he arrived, I paid him with my card. As I put my bag in the back of my jeep and took a deep, steadying breath, I glanced back at the Eight Ball Motel, hoping I would never see this place again. I got in my car and started it.

I'd thought the eight-hour drive from Jacksonville to Kansas had been bad, but this twelve-hour trip was killing me. I was going stir crazy. Finally, my GPS told me my destination was only thirty minutes away. I looked around and saw all the beautiful mountains and the fog. It was breathtaking. Sure, Florida was beautiful, but this was a different type of beauty altogether. It was a relaxing, out-of-a-dream kind of beautiful.

At long last, I pulled up to Bluntin College. It reminded me of an old English castle. Ten solid round towers were perched around the main part of the college, all connected by gray cobblestone walls. Stained glass windows were scattered across the college buildings. I was greeted by two twenty-foot metal gates, which opened slowly to let me in. Bluntin College was one of the oldest colleges in Colorado, and it was, indeed, the best, especially for history degrees.

When I arrived at my dorm—number 201, on the second floor—I was completely and utterly exhausted. I just brought up one bag for the time being. After the painfully long drive, I didn't think I could bring up anymore.

The room was no bigger than fifty square feet, and it housed two beds, one on each side. All the lights were off, and it was quiet. I wasn't sure if my roommate was in, so I didn't turn the light on. I stumbled across the floor to the nearest empty bed and lay there, facedown, telling myself I would get up in ten minutes and take a shower. But my eyes were too heavy, and my body was too exhausted, and I soon fell asleep.

CHAPTER 3
COLLEGE LIFE

I heard a banging noise, followed by the sound of someone saying, "Oh my God. Please don't tell me you're a druggie."

I rolled over, half asleep, my eyes still half shut.

Then I heard a loud "Hello!"

I slowly and reluctantly opened my eyes and sat up, only to see a bright-eyed and bushy-tailed blond girl with big blue eyes and round black glasses. "Yes," I managed to say.

"Yes what?" she said. "You're a druggie. Oh, God. I can't deal with this."

I rubbed my head, trying to wake up. "No, I'm not. I'm an exhausted eighteen-year-old woman who just got startled awake."

She was clearly taken aback. "Well, excuse me. Most people I know that go to Bluntin College wouldn't be sleeping in the clothes they arrived in on the morning of the first day of school. They'd be up and ready to start their day, especially since most classes start in twenty minutes," she snapped as she pushed her glasses up her nose.

I jumped up quicker than my brain had time to process. "What time is it?" I said frantically.

"It's twenty past nine," she said with confusion on her face. "Anyway," she continued as I scurried about the room, opening my bag and running to the bathroom. "My name is Caroline. I'm your new dorm buddy. Lucky you. I'm a sophomore here, and I take my academics very seriously, which is why I requested a roommate who would take their academics seriously too." She sighed. "But I guess all we can do is hope for the best, right? Well, I'm off to class. I hope you have a great first day."

I grumbled a thanks, which seemed to placate her, and she left.

I hurried to take a quick shower, brush my teeth, brush my hair, and change my clothes. By some miracle, I was out the door by 9:35 a.m. My first class was Composition One in classroom 313. I rushed into the classroom at 9:40 a.m. Keeping my head down, not wanting to make eye contact with anyone, I searched for a seat in the back. When I finally spotted an empty desk, I dropped my books on it and threw myself into the chair.

I looked up when the professor started talking. He was a tall, thin man with gray hair and a small goatee. He looked very serious, but he had a certain lightheartedness about him. "Good morning, class. Welcome to Composition One. Here, you will begin developing the skills you'll need to succeed in life." He paused. "Well, to write a decent paper, at least." He smiled, and a couple of students laughed.

I scanned the classroom. There were about twenty students. Most of them looked young like me, but there were a couple of older women, who sat next to each other, looking apprehensive. The professor was about to start speaking again when the door opened with a loud creak.

Three men came in, laughing. The first one was a dark-haired boy with brown eyes and one dimple on his left cheek; he was about six foot two. The second seemed a little more serious; he had the air of someone who had seen a lot in life, and when he smiled with his friends, it didn't seem to reach his eyes. The last of the men had bright red hair. I did a doubletake. It was Lou. He looked different than he had when I'd met him at the motel. His hair was gelled and styled, and he wore a football jacket with the school logo on it. Almost immediately, he caught me looking at him.

"Mr. Blakely, what an honor it is for you to join us today. To what do I owe the pleasure of you disrupting my class in the middle of a lecture?" the professor asked condescendingly.

Lou smiled. "My deepest apologies, sir. My fellow classmates were lost. They needed some help to find your class. I obliged."

The professor shot him an agitated look. "I see. Please do tell your classmates that if they disrupt my class again, they can stay where they were."

"But of course." Lou flashed an innocent smile.

The other two men sat opposite each other about three seats away from me. When I looked up, I found Lou looking at me. He smiled, then walked out.

Well, isn't he chivalrous? If a little bold, I thought.

The professor continued to talk for about an hour before giving us our homework assignments. After Composition One, I went to my math class, just managing to stay awake for the hour-and-a-half lesson.

After class, I decided to go to the school cafeteria to get some coffee and a muffin. I found a spot by the window where I could people-watch and drink my coffee. My next class wasn't for another thirty minutes. I watched all the different people that walked by, and I wondered what their lives were like. I wondered if how they looked reflected how they truly felt. I knew that when my mother had died, I'd plastered a smile on my face, but inside, I'd felt like I was dying. You never knew what someone was going through; people were good at putting on a mask.

For some reason, I'd never really felt connected to people. Sometimes, it felt like I was just going through the motions of life. Even though I felt like I was supposed to be doing something more, I didn't know what it was. I hoped becoming an archeologist would change these feelings.

I took another sip of my coffee and was about to get up when I saw a girl no taller than five-foot three slip and fall, spilling her drink all over herself and dropping her notes on the floor. She looked mortified; I was mortified for her.

A couple of girls snickered, and a couple of guys put their hands over their mouths, chuckling.

I got up and ran over to her. "Are you okay?" I asked.

"Yeah, I'm fine. I just don't know what's wrong with me. I'm so clumsy," she said in frustration.

I helped her up and started picking up her papers. "We all have our moments," I told her with a feeble smile.

She looked at me. "Yeah, but my moments always seem to be catastrophes." She looked around, blushing.

"I've seen worse," I told her. I handed her the last piece of paper.

She blew her bangs out of her face. "Really?" she asked with desperation in her voice.

"Really." I smiled at her.

"Well, my name is Madeline, and I appreciate you coming to my rescue. I'm a freshman from Kansas."

I laughed to myself, thinking about my horrible experience at the Kansas motel.

She asked me what I was laughing about.

I explained that I'd had a bad experience in Kansas.

"Yeah, Kansas is no place to go if you don't know anyone. It can be pretty tough, not to mention boring."

She asked me what my schedule was and told me hers. We didn't have any classes together, but we were both taking Composition One. We talked a bit more about our classes and exchanged numbers. Then I had to leave to make it to my next class. So far, school was turning out pretty well, and college wasn't as hard as I'd been expecting it to be. It was almost like high school, though the people were bigger and louder.

My first week of college went well. I became friends with Madeline, and I got all my work done on time. I even got a job helping the swim team with their equipment. Things were looking pretty good for me.

"All right, guppies," said Coach Hurtle. "Pack it up. You guys did well today."

There were about five girls and ten guys on the Bluntin College swim team, which was one of the top swim teams in the country. They all tossed their towels and goggles to me. I gathered them and took them into the locker room, putting the towels in the washer and cleaning the googles. I finished with thirty minutes to go before the pool closed, so I decided to change into my bathing suit and take a quick swim.

The pool was beautiful, one of the biggest pools I'd ever seen. As I stepped into the water, I thought to myself that this was exactly what I needed. I took a breath and launched my body into the water, into the blissful silence. The feeling of weightlessness hit me, and I felt calm. Then zing! An odd sensation jolted through my body. My eyes flew open. I tried to swim to the surface, but it felt like something was holding my leg, keeping me in the water. I looked down; nothing was there. But still, I was stuck in the middle of the pool, sinking like a rock.

I swore I could hear muffled speech coming from the bottom of the pool. "Go home. Go home."

Finally, whatever had a hold on my foot released it. I swam to the surface, gasping for air and coughing desperately. I looked around and saw two women swimming in the deep end, whispering to each other and giggling. I then noticed two men sitting on the side, their feet in the water, in deep conversation. One of them looked at me, a hint of concern on his face, but he continued to talk to his friend.

I swam to the steps, where I sat down, resting my hands on my knees. "What's wrong with me?" I whispered to myself.

"Rose?"

The sound of my name being called startled me out of my thoughts. I turned around to see Lou in his swimming trunks, looking like he'd climbed right out of a swim magazine. I took a deep breath and gave him a weak smile.

He walked faster toward me. "Are you okay?"

I nodded. "Yes. For some reason, I just got stuck under the water. Maybe a leg cramp or something."

Lou smiled. "And I thought you girls from Florida were supposed to be some of the best swimmers." He took a seat next to me.

I took a deep breath and looked up at him. "I'm good enough to beat you," I said with one eyebrow raised. I didn't know what had gotten into me. Maybe it was the lack of oxygen to my brain.

"Is that a challenge I hear?" he asked, a wide grin on his face.

I grinned back. "It looks like guys from Kentucky aren't as dull as I'd heard."

"You shouldn't believe everything you hear." Lou jumped into the pool. "On the count of three, we start. Whoever makes it there and back first wins."

Surprisingly, Lou beat me by a landslide. He was a lot faster than I'd given him credit for.

As I tried to catch my breath, I sputtered out, "How did you get so fast?"

Lou started laughing. "I was on the swim team last year, but I decided to give it up to focus on my grades."

I coughed. "You were on the swim team?"

He shot me a smile. "Does that surprise you?"

I started stuttering, realizing too late that I might have offended him. "I just thought you looked more like—"

He interrupted me. "A football player," he finished. "No. Too much physical contact for me."

As Lou spoke, I realized how comfortable I was with him. He reminded me a lot of Tyler. I usually wasn't so friendly and talkative with new people, but there was something about him that made me feel relaxed and at ease.

"You know, you shouldn't judge a book by its cover," he said. "We're probably more alike than you think."

I blushed a little, feeling a tad guilty for being judgmental.

He laughed. "It's okay. I would think the same thing. I do have pretty big muscles." He flexed proudly.

I rolled my eyes at him and told him I had to go. "The pool is closing. I'll see you around."

"Hey, Rose. What are you doing next Friday?"

I smiled. "Besides school and cleaning goggles, nothing."

"Do you want to go to a small party?" Lou asked.

I laughed, shaking my head. "I'm sorry. I'm not the party type. Believe it or not, I'm quite an introvert."

"I believe it," Lou replied, "but you'll be with me." He put on a charming smile that showed his perfect white teeth.

"Maybe another time," I said, walking back to the locker room to change.

When I arrived back at my dorm, Caroline was on her computer, typing away. Upon seeing me, she closed her laptop and began talking. "So, how was your first week? I haven't seen you much." Her voice lilted happily. Caroline always seemed to be in an upbeat mood; I wished I had her energy.

I sighed. I wanted to get in the shower, and I knew this was going to be a long conversation. "It was nice," I said as I sat down on my bed.

I looked around the dorm. It really was small; we didn't have much space. The beds on each side were twins, and we had enough room for one small dresser each. We were lucky enough to have a sink, some cabinet space, and a microwave. We also had a mini fridge to put our food in. Luckily, I mostly ate frozen dinners, so I didn't take up much space.

I cast my gaze to Caroline's side of the room. It was perfectly neat, decorated with a pink bedspread, flower paintings, and glowing fairy lights. It was very chic, just like something out of a magazine. I couldn't help but admire her eye for design.

Caroline looked at me, fingers tapping on her closed laptop. She clearly wanted more detail.

"My week went well," I told her. "I got a job helping with the swim team, and my grades are pretty good. I like college so far," I said with a genuine smile.

Wow, I thought to myself. *Look at me opening up to my roommate, racing guys in the pool, and getting good grades. I cannot believe who I'm becoming*. In high school, I'd always kept to myself. I'd never made many friends, other than Tyler; I'd been the quiet girl who no one seemed to notice.

Caroline smiled back. "That is so awesome. My first week has been cool too. I'm getting all A's in my classes, of course," she said matter-of-factly. "But the people this year seem to be so much happier." Her eyes shone. "I even met somebody."

I raised an eyebrow. "Oh, really?"

Caroline didn't seem like the type to get into relationships. She was too focused on school; she wanted to be a doctor. Her face gleamed with excitement. "Yes! He's really sweet, and he's studying to become a physician." She gave a heaving sigh. "Do you believe in love at first sight?" she asked, eyeing her flower paintings.

I couldn't help but laugh.

She gave me a side glance, eyes narrowed. "What's so funny?"

"I'm sorry," I said earnestly. "I didn't mean to laugh out loud." As I got up, took one of my microwave meals out of the freezer, and popped it into the microwave, I began to talk. "Love at first sight isn't something I've ever experienced, so I'd have to say no. I don't believe in it."

Caroline nodded sharply, then looked back at the flower painting on the wall. "Just because you've never experienced something doesn't mean it's not true."

I typed in the time on the microwave, folded my arms across my chest, and thought about what she'd said.

Caroline opened her laptop and began typing again, a faint smile on her face.

I ate my microwave dinner, then took a shower and headed to bed.

That night, my dreams were unlike any I'd had before. They felt so real. It was like I was in another dimension. I was by myself in the water, searching for somebody, searching for something. I saw my mother standing about twenty feet from me, trying to tell me something, a worried expression on her face.

I was running to her as fast as I could through the water, but the closer I got, the less she looked like my mother. Though the figure still had my mother's face, there were long black octopus arms coming out of her. Her mouth was moving, speaking to me. "Come home. Come home," she said over and over again.

When I got close to her face, everything melted away, and in my mother's place was a creature with green eyes and black octopus arms. It grabbed me, binding me so I couldn't move. I couldn't think. I couldn't breathe. I felt like I had died.

I woke up gasping for air, drenched in sweat. I rolled to the side of my bed and shook my head.

Caroline grumbled something in her sleep and turned over.

I walked fast to the bathroom and took a couple of deep breaths as I looked in the mirror. I examined my reflection. My black hair was stuck to my face, and my nightshirt was completely drenched in sweat. I splashed my face with water and took some more deep, calming breaths. What was happening to me? I didn't feel stressed. There wasn't any pressure on me. So why did I have such anxiety? Was it that my mother's death was still affecting me? I thought I'd come to terms with it.

I decided to take a quick shower in the hope that it would help me relax a bit. As I stood under the water,

I heard a hissing sound. I froze, still as a deer being hunted. Eyes wide, heart pumping, I stood still and silent for a minute. I didn't hear anything further, so I continued to shower, letting the warm water calm me.

As soon as I relaxed, I heard the sound again, but this time, it sounded like it was saying something. "Come," it hissed.

I turned off the shower and slowly looked behind the curtain. Nothing and no one. I shook my head. *I just need a good night's rest*, I told myself. I dried my hair and got back into bed. I was too exhausted to think too much about the sound. I let sleep take me over and decided to worry about it in the morning.

CHAPTER 4

THE PARTY

One of my favorite things about Saturdays was that there was no need for an alarm clock. I woke up to the soft sound of Caroline typing on her laptop. I felt so much better now that I'd gotten some sleep, so much so that I almost forgot about the horrible dream I'd had during the night. Almost.

"Good morning, sleepyhead," Caroline said in a peppy voice. "Or should I say good afternoon." She set her laptop on her bed and got up. "Have any plans for this weekend?"

Still trying to wake up, I grunted a no as I put my feet down on the floor.

She gave me a look of distaste. "You know, I have to say, I've never seen someone look so much like they've been through hell and high water when they wake up. You take the cake."

"Thanks," I said in a sarcastic tone as I dragged myself to the bathroom.

I looked at myself in the mirror and inwardly chuckled. Caroline was right. My hair was a tangled mess, there was crust in my eyes, and my lips were very chapped. I splashed water on my face and brushed my teeth and hair.

When I walked out, I noticed Caroline making googly eyes at her phone, a goofy smile on her face. Ah, the infatuation stage. I remembered girls in high school talking about the boys they liked and showing their friends text messages with that same look on their faces. I was happy for Caroline.

I decided this weekend was going to be all about getting my papers done. I had a big paper due for my comp class on Monday, and I was going to need all the energy and focus I had to finish it. Bluntin College was living up to its reputation for being one of the hardest academic colleges. Their grading criteria was no joke, but it only motivated me.

Before I knew it, it was Monday morning again. I woke up feeling sluggish and tired. No matter how much sleep I got, I never felt completely rested. Class went by slowly. I fought to keep my eyes open and pay as much attention as possible.

Tuesday and Wednesday passed by in a blur, but when Thursday arrived, there seemed to be an energy moving around the school. Everybody was buzzing. I guessed there was a big football game on Friday night and a lot of afterparties that everyone was looking forward to. People were passing out flyers, girls were giggling more than usual, and guys seemed louder and broodier.

I went to the cafeteria to get some food and coffee, hoping they'd give me some energy. As I waited in line, I saw a bright red apple, and my stomach grumbled. I'd never been a big fruit eater, but sometimes, you have to listen to what your body is telling you. I paid for the apple and a coffee, then sat down in my favorite seat by the window.

I started to think about the dream I'd had again. Soon, though, my thoughts were interrupted by the thud of books landing on the table I was sitting at. I looked up to see Madeline.

She scowled, looking frustrated. "I swear, I have the worst luck," she huffed and sat down across from me.

I gave her a concerned look. "What's going on?"

"Well, for starters, Mr. Charles gave me a C-minus on my paper because he hates me."

I hid my smirk. From what I could tell, Madeline was a procrastinator, and she wasn't the best at writing.

"Granted," she continued, "there were a couple of teeny-tiny mistakes, but overall, it was a solid B paper for sure. I think he hates me because I remind him of his ex-wife."

I tried hard to bite back a laugh.

She looked at me incredulously. "I'm serious! I saw a picture of her. I look just like her. I mean, of course, I'm a little better looking, and I'm younger, but still, the resemblance is there." Madeline's hair bounced around her face as she continued to talk about how Mr. Charles had it out for her. Madeline might have looked like she was all about school and learning, but she was quite the personality and a firecracker at that. She had fiery red hair, hazel eyes, and a few freckles sprinkled across her nose. She dressed in jeans and big sweaters a lot, but she sometimes changed it up and dressed very elegantly. Today was a sweater and jeans kind of day. "And then," she said, exasperated, "I'm supposed to go to this party tonight at the Beta Phi house, but Janine completely bailed on me." She threw her hands up. "What kind of friend does that? I barely have a social life as it is. She knows I won't go by myself. Like, seriously, who would go by themselves to a frat boy party?"

I looked out the window and tried not to make eye contact with her. I did not want her to ask me to go.

I wasn't the type to enjoy myself around big groups of young adults, let alone drunk ones. Plus, I had a date with my bed and a movie.

There was a stretch of silence that lasted about thirty seconds before I heard "Rose" in a sweet tone that was laced with persuasiveness.

"Madeline," I responded emotionlessly.

"Rose, we have been the closest of friends for two weeks now, and that means a great deal to me. I mean, you practically saved my life. I could have died of embarrassment." She batted her eyelashes.

I shot her an exasperated look. "As sweet as that is of you to say, I can't go. I don't do well at social events. I'm an introvert, very antisocial," I said with a plea in my eyes.

"Rose," she groaned, getting ready to state her defense. "You don't even have to be social! I just need you to go with me for an hour and a half. If you want to bail after that, that's fine. You don't have to drink, and you don't have to talk to anybody. It'll be good for you to see the rest of the campus. You've only seen your dorm and classes." She threw her hands up in the air again for emphasis. "Don't you want to explore the rest of the college and see what's out there?" She paused for a minute, but when I didn't answer, she pressed on. "You know, if you really want to be an archeologist, you're going to have to be a little bit more adventurous," she challenged.

I slouched back in my chair and crossed my arms over my chest. I had finished all my homework, and I supposed an hour wouldn't be so bad, just as long as people didn't bombard me. Who was I kidding? People barely even noticed me! I looked up at Madeline.

She was still staring at me, hope in her eyes and a victorious smile on her lips. "Please," she said, knowing I was on the verge of breaking.

I took a deep breath. "I know I'm going to regret this, but I'll go for one hour," I said sternly.

Madeline made an excited squeaky noise. "You will not regret this! This is going to be the best night of your life! I just don't know what to wear. I've got to get everything together." She scooped her books up. "I'm going to text you. I owe you."

I shook my head and gave her a nod. I couldn't believe I was doing this.

Madeline turned back to me. "Oh, you have to wear red. It's part of the Beta tradition, apparently."

I nodded again, watching as she skipped out of the cafeteria.

After I finished my last class, I started thinking about the party and quickly became very anxious. I chewed my nails as I walked to my dorm.

When I opened the door, I found Caroline standing in front of her mirror in a short red dress and black flats. She turned to look at me, her makeup flawless and her curls bouncier than ever. She smiled.

I gave her a half-smile back.

"Guess where I'm going," she said in a happy-go-lucky tone.

As I got my stuff ready for the shower, I said, "The Beta Phi party."

She sounded a little disappointed. "How did you know?"

"Just a lucky guess," I grumbled as I walked to the shower and shut the door.

"Aren't you in a foul mood?" I heard her say as she started rummaging through her drawers.

I turned on the shower and took a deep breath. *One hour*, I thought. *It couldn't be that bad*. If I could handle Tyler's eighteenth birthday party for two hours, I could do this for one. I took a long shower and some deep breaths, and I found a long-sleeve red shirt and a pair of dark-wash jeans. It was a little chilly out, so I brought a sweater as well. When I finished getting ready, I lay on my bed and was about to open up my laptop to check some work when I heard a knock on the door. I looked at the clock; it was 7:59 already.

I opened the door to see Madeline in one of the prettiest red dresses I'd ever seen. It was form-fitting, stopping below her knee, and it had a lace design all over it. It hugged all the right places on Madeline's frame. She had her hair half up, half down, and she was wearing red lipstick.

"Wow," I said. "You look great, Madeline."

She beamed with pride.

Caroline came up behind me. "Excuse me," she said. She stopped to look at Madeline, then back at me. "You look lovely," she said. "Maybe a tad overdressed, but you look lovely as a dove." She looked Madeline and up and down one more time, then walked out. Caroline was never afraid to speak her mind.

Madeline looked at me. "Well, she's 'lovely as a dove,'" she said, raising her hands to make quotation marks in the air. She laughed.

We began walking to the Beta Phi house, and Madeline told me I should try to spruce up a little bit more when going to parties. I looked down at my red shirt and pants and asked her what was wrong with what I was wearing, but she just huffed and continued walking without offering me an answer.

We got to the Beta Phi house in five minutes; it was across the street from the school. There were cars parked for miles, and loud music blared from the house. It was so much worse than I could ever have expected. People were already beyond drunk, some even laying passed out on the front lawn. I looked up at Madeline and gave her a look, then started to turn around, but she grabbed my arm and rushed us to the door, knocking three times, then two times, then four.

A six-foot-tall guy with short black hair and big brown eyes dressed in a red sweatshirt and dark jeans opened the door. He licked his lips and gave Madeline and me an approving smile. "Drinks in the kitchen, games in the back, and upstairs if you want to have some real fun." He shot us a grin.

I turned my head to the right, pretending I'd seen something interesting happening on the other side of the house. It was a technique I'd learned to avoid conversations or awkward situations with people.

"Thanks," Madeline said with a flirty smile. Then she turned to me. "You drinking?"

"No thanks," I said.

"Go get us seats in the back, then. I'll bring you some punch." She slipped away into the crowd.

The house smelled like sweat and cheap cologne. The music was booming, and it was so crowded that I could barely make out what anyone was saying. I crossed one arm over my body and began to work my way through the crowd. I got bumped three times, earned a couple of funny looks from some girls, and had one guy grab my arm before I was able to find a seat. "This is exactly why I do not come to parties," I grumbled to myself.

The back was where the drinking games were taking place. There was a little table with three chairs that nobody had claimed yet. I rushed over, but before I could sit down, someone set two cups of punch down. I looked up to see who it was. Lou. I took a deep breath and smiled at him, happy to see a familiar face. "I can't believe you showed up."

"Who was the lucky person who convinced you to come?" Lou asked.

I let out a half-laugh. "How do you know I didn't come by myself?"

He raised an eyebrow. "Did you?"

I sat down, sighed, and admitted that I'd come with my friend Madeline.

Lou sat down across from me and pushed one of the cups into my hand. "I brought you a punch," he said with a charming smile. "Nonalcoholic, of course." He winked.

"I'm glad you know me so well," I said, accepting it.

He nodded. "I would expect nothing less."

I gave him a disapproving look. "I suspect yours is nonalcoholic too," I said facetiously.

He took a big gulp. "Well, one of us has to have some fun."

I smiled a little. I was feeling a little lightheaded, so I took a big sip from my cup, hoping the sugar would help.

Lou asked me how my classes were going and how I was liking college life.

"My classes are going great," I told him. "I really enjoy …" Before I could finish my sentence, I noticed Lou's mouth flickering. Big, then small. Big, then small. I shut my eyes and lifted my hand to my head.

"Are you okay?" Lou asked in a concerned voice.

"Yeah," I said, squinting my eyes and rubbing my head. "I probably just didn't eat enough today." This was a lie, and I knew it. I'd eaten a lot, but maybe it hadn't been as much as I'd thought. I opened my eyes, desperately hoping that everything would be back to normal, but instead, not only was Lou's mouth bigger, but there were colors everywhere, colors I had never seen in my life, colors I couldn't even explain because I hadn't known they existed. They bounced all around Lou. "Are you sure you got me a nonalcoholic drink?" I asked. I could feel anxiety building in my chest.

Before Lou could answer, a tall, dark figure walked over and put a hand on his shoulder. Lou's face grew very stern, and he didn't say a word.

I looked up at the black figure and tried to make out a face through all the colors dancing around my vision. All I saw was a big hand. He leaned in closer to me, putting his long, strong arm over the statue-like Lou.

It was him. The perfect man from the motel. My anxiety hit a new high.

We sat in silence for about fifteen seconds, his light-brown eyes examining every part of my face and body with an intense stare.

My heart was fluttering, but it wasn't just from the anxiety. There was something about him that made my heartbeat faster.

"Get up," he said emotionlessly.

"Excuse me?" I managed to sputter out. The colors were growing thicker, and his presence was overwhelming. My chest felt light and warm.

He sighed as if agitated. "Get up," he repeated, slower and sterner this time.

As I watched his mouth move, I saw blue mixed with pink and purple pour out of his mouth. Yellow danced all around him, and there was a tinge of blue on his chest, over his heart.

Lou must have given me a drink spiked with alcohol, or even worse, something else. I'd thought he was my friend, someone I could trust. But I would not let this man see my weakness. I wouldn't let him know what was going on in my head. Who did he think he was to boss me around? I didn't even know him.

I crossed my arms in defiance and sat back. "No," I said. Then fear pierced my heart. Something wasn't right. Something was going on. I could feel it.

He smiled as if amused. Within a blink, he was five inches away from my face. His eyes were like dancing starlight mixed with honey and all my deepest desires.

I could feel his warmth on my skin. I hadn't realized how cold I was until he'd come this close. His warmth consumed me, making me feel relaxed even when I didn't want it to.

His once amused eyes now held concern. "Do you trust me?" he asked with sincerity in his voice.

"What?" My mind screamed no, but the look in his eyes and the concern in his voice touched something deep inside of me. My head nodded yes almost of its own accord. *What was that?* I wondered.

"The truth of your soul defiles your lies," he said, a challenging look in his eyes. He grabbed my hand.

I looked at Lou, whose eyes stared blankly ahead. Still, he did not move.

CHAPTER 5

HIM

Beautiful blue light surrounded him. Everything was a blur. We started walking fast. My feet wouldn't stop, my mind was confused by the colors everywhere, and I couldn't make out what was real or fake. His brisk walked turned into a jog. I couldn't keep up, but then his hand was on my waist, holding me as he ran. Why couldn't I control the movement of my legs? Part of me wanted to fight, but another part a part of me didn't. His hands around my waist felt comforting and grounding, and I felt so out of control.

The further away we got from the party, the more the colors faded, and reality started setting in. He stopped in front of a black car and opened the door without saying anything.

I sat down, still dazed and confused.

He took the seatbelt and put it on me.

"I've got it," I said, but he didn't listen.

He buckled me in, closed the door, and climbed into the driver's seat. He started the car, and by that time, my senses had fully kicked in. My head started spinning, not only with dizziness but with questions.

Before I could bombard him with the thoughts spinning through my head, the beautiful man began to talk. "Are you feeling okay?" he asked in a concerned and surprisingly soft voice.

I turned to look at him, shocked. His voice seemed different than it had in all the other encounters I'd had with him. I wondered if he knew what was going on with me, if he knew if I had been drugged or what I'd drunk. He could see that I was going through something. "I don't know," I stuttered.

The once bright yellow starlight and swirling neon blue in his eyes started to dim and fade back to that beautiful honey brown. He turned the heat on and pointed it all toward me. In a soft voice, as he tightened his jaw, he said, "Tell me what you see. Tell me what you feel and see." He clenched the leather steering wheel tightly.

It took me about thirty seconds to get my thoughts together. "Well, I feel very confused," I said, then paused. Could I trust this man and tell him the truth about what I was going through?

As if he knew how I was feeling, he looked me in the eyes and said, "You can trust me."

I fidgeted with the seatbelt and took a deep breath. I was already in the car with him, so I felt like there was nothing to lose. "I'm seeing colors," I said. "Not normal colors. Colors I've never seen before. I thought maybe Lou did give me a drink with alcohol, or maybe someone slipped something in my drink. But this is different." I paused again and huffed. "You won't understand. It's unexplainable. It's starting to go away now anyway," I said, my voice growing quiet.

He was silent for a moment, staring out at the road. Then he spoke again. "I understand more than you know."

"Where are we going?" I asked him. "Do you know what happened? Did you see someone put something in my drink?" *That must have been it*, I thought.

He took the next turn, and we were at the back of the college. He put the car in park, then looked at me. He reached out like he was about to touch me.

I closed my eyes and braced myself.

When I opened my eyes again, he was close to my face. I could taste his breath, like cool winter nights. He unbuckled my seatbelt, and I looked into his eyes. They knocked the breath right out of me. He had to have been the most attractive man I had ever seen. My heart began to flutter. I felt like I was in a trance I never wanted to get out of.

"You have a choice, Rose," he said in a soft and sympathetic voice. He paused as if trying to find the right words to say. "You are about to experience some big changes. They are through no fault of your own. Sometimes, life gives us a certain destiny, and we have no choice but to follow it."

My heart was starting to beat faster.

"I have been following you for the last month to see if you are one of us."

My heart almost jumped out of my chest. But I stayed silent.

He was very careful when he talked. He spoke with elegance and poise. "I will start by saying that your drink was not spiked. It was a potion." He looked into my eyes so penetratingly that I felt like he could see my soul, like he knew my heart was fluttering. "There is nothing you can do to stop the changes that are coming. The potion was meant to expose who you truly are." He paused as if searching for something, then continued. "As I stated before, you have a choice. You can come home with me, and I will get you home safe and protect you. Or you can stay here, and I will protect you, but they will come for you. They will want to take you home. You can go with another, and I will follow."

I felt a wash of relief as I realized that the thing that remained consistent in all my choices was that he was in them. I tried to process what he was explaining to me.

He waited patiently, looking at me the entire time, analyzing me.

I finally whispered, "Where is home?"

He seemed taken aback by my question, but he still spoke calmly and assertively. "Argathia," he said, watching my reaction intently.

I sighed. "I figured it wasn't going to be somewhere I knew. Where is that?"

He answered immediately. It was like he'd known already that that was what I was going to say. "Inner Earth," he declared, gazing intently into my eyes.

"Why do I need to go to Argathia?" I asked nervously. "And why do you want to take me there? Obviously, you're not too fond of me," I said in a tone that came off more hurt than I intended it to.

He moved so quickly that it startled me. He was so close to my face that I could make out the pores in his skin. His warmth took over my coldness. His eyes locked fiercely on mine. He began to speak with anger in his tone, but even laced with anger, his words came out like a soft melody. "You represent everything I stand for, everything my heart stands for," he said.

I kept my eyes locked with his, feeling hazy from the warmth of his presence. It felt like I was sitting under the sun, being caressed by its warm rays. I could sit here just like this all day.

He closed his eyes and took a deep breath. Then he leaned back, taking his warmth with him.

I put my arms around myself, feeling the cold again.

"I'm sorry," he said in a whisper.

"For what?" I stammered out.

"I shouldn't have …" He stopped for a second. "I can't get too close to you without … connecting with your essence."

I looked at him with confusion in my eyes.

He turned his head and looked out the window, bringing his hands to his lips. "We are all made up of essence, some more than others. Some have light essence. Others have dark. Argathia is made up of the essence of the Earth and the essence of humans. Most beings from Inner Earth need essence to survive, especially if we are in Outer Earth for too long. We begin to need essence more, and we can become sick if we don't get it."

I watched him talk, entranced by his beauty. It was hard for me to concentrate, but I was trying my best.

Everything he said was spoken with fervor. "Human essence gives us more strength and sometimes power," he continued. "We have craved it more and more over the centuries."

When I heard centuries, my head jerked up from his mouth to his eyes. I saw a tinge of amusement in them at my reaction.

"Yes," he said. "Centuries."

I started fidgeting with my seatbelt, quiet for a minute.

He stared out into the night, looking like he was about to say something.

"I choose you," I told him in a voice that I wanted to sound assuring but instead sounded more emotional than anything else.

He turned to me slowly, confused.

"I want you to take me," I continued.

His face was still serious, but his eyes danced with happiness. "I'm eternally grateful," he told me.

My mind was racing frantically. "I do have some questions."

"Anything," he said, his voice thick with emotion.

"Why must I go home, as you say? Why can't I live here?"

He nodded as if agreeing with my question. "Your mother was from Argathia," he explained. "She was not human. In Argathia, there are traditions and rules that must be followed, no matter what. You are part of their species, and that means that you must make a choice: to stay there and choose a tribe or fight to leave."

My heart would not stop racing. We agreed to go to my dorm to get my stuff.

As we walked down the hall, I was aware of his presence behind me, a comfort when everything else made me anxious. He was in sync with me and with every step I took.

I opened the door to my dorm, hoping Caroline wasn't inside. To my surprise, she wasn't. I gave a sigh of relief. Something about the room felt different. It was colder than it usually was, the air stale and still. I turned on the light, and before I could pull my hand back, the man who still had not told me his name grabbed my waist and pulled me close behind him. "Show yourself, Sapien," he growled in a voice I could never have imagined would come from such a beautiful man.

Fear struck my heart. I didn't know if it was from the sound of his voice or from the enormous hooded black figure that sprung to life ten inches from his face moments later. If I'd had any doubts about whether or not this was not real, they were destroyed at that very moment.

The hooded figure hissed at him. "How dare you utter my name, you peasant!" it spat out, its voice filled with hatred.

He pulled me closer to him. His warmth crushed into me and gave me a slither of comfort, but I remained frozen in fear.

The hooded creature continued spitting words laced with venom. "You dare defile the traditions of our forefathers."

"I defile nothing," he said with authority. "I am bringing her to Argathia." He took a step closer to the hooded figure.

The figure hissed in anger. "It is not your place to make such decisions." It moved its arms, looking ready to strike.

Now I was scared for him. My fear for his life overtook my fear for mine. I pushed myself out from behind him. "I choose to go with him," I said in a voice I barely recognized; it was bold and strong, not betraying the overwhelming fear I felt.

The figure jerked its head to look at me.

The beautiful man grabbed me gently and pushed me closer to his side.

The figure still hissed, but it was quieter now. "You are a child," it told me. "You know nothing of what you want or who you are."

I puffed out my chest. "I choose him to take me." That was all I could manage. My hands were shaking, and the thickness of the air was making it hard to breathe.

The figure stood there and looked at me. I could not see its face, for its hood covered everything, but I could tell it wasn't pleased.

"Leave," my protector said in an inhuman growl.

"If you dishonor the traditions of your forefathers," the figure hissed, "you will pay." With that, the figure slowly faded out, green eyes glaring from under its hood until it had disappeared completely.

I took in a deep breath of air.

The man spun around. "Are you all right?" he asked, looking at my face, then surveying my body, analyzing me.

I blushed deeply.

He caught my eyes. "Please," he said, clenching his jaw and looking away from me, "don't ever do that again. You don't know what he could have done to you." He drew a deep breath. "I couldn't live with myself if anything happened to you."

I didn't know why I did it—it was like a compulsion—but I grabbed his cheek and turned his head to me.

He backed away gently. "I don't trust myself," he said, shame in his voice.

I stepped closer so that I was mere inches from his face, enveloped in his warmth. "I trust you," I said. I looked into his eyes, where flickers of blue danced between depths of honey brown.

"Grab anything that's important to you," he said in a rushed tone.

I didn't have much. I filled my bag with whatever I could, though, not caring what I ended up with. Emotions bubbled up inside of me.

"You're going to be okay. I'll make sure of it," the man said as if reading my mind.

"I'm fine." I tried not to let my voice rise in pitch.

"You're not a very good liar," he told me. "Your emotions are given away by your face and through your energy."

I blushed and tried to redirect the conversation. "Well, why was there an eight-foot hooded creature in my room?"

He looked at me as he zipped up my backpack and swung it over one of his shoulders. His tone grew soft. "There's not much time. I'll tell you as we walk."

I could tell he was in a rush, but he never once rushed me. His steps imitated mine even though he was much taller and had a naturally longer stride. After a few moments had passed, he began talking, breaking the silence. "You have a warrant on you, for lack of a better term."

That made me speed up my pace a bit. "A warrant?" I coughed in disbelief.

He stared straight ahead, but his arms were touching mine, which offered me some comfort.

I willed myself to focus, not to let the touch of skin distract me. "Why do I have a warrant on me?"

He looked confused but kept talking. "Argathia was made of three tribes," he explained, speaking with elegance and precision, as though every word was carefully chosen. His tone was firm but pleasant. "The Argathians, the Luthernians, and the Sapiens. But now there are only two tribes left: the Luthernians and the Sapiens. All the tribes are from different places and times. They decided to come together and create a second home in Inner Earth, where they each could rule. The current Luthernian king is King Demondae. He was the son of Lord Cabrakkan, who had many different wives. Cabrakkan was a wicked lord who treated his wives poorly. He believed females were worth less than males, and he belittled them, even going as far as to torture one of his wives almost to the point of death." He clenched his jaw tightly.

"Lord Cabrakkan had three equals: Lord Sapien, Lord Olorus, and Lord Bakusura." He paused, looking at me briefly before pressing on. "Olorus and Bakusura shared one kingdom and were never fond of Lord Cabrakkan. Lord Olorus fell in love with an Argathian woman and produced a daughter, who he loved with his whole heart. That was when everything changed. Olorus began to despise Lord Cabrakkan for the way he treated women in his kingdom, for even though they were separate, the three rulers all crossed paths. The last straw was when Lord Cabrakkan talked down to Olorus's daughter. But Olorus was limited in terms of what he could do, for the original scroll they had all signed had rules."

I looked up at him incredulously. "What rules?"

He sighed. "There were five original rules of the lords. First, each lord was allowed a kingdom to rule as they pleased. Second, they were not to tell humans about Argathia. Third, if one of the lords did not like the way another was ruling, he could challenge him to a daji. Fourth, the offspring of the lords were to have the same rights as the lords themselves. And fifth, the firstborn child of each lord would inherit their father's kingdom when he died. Olorus tried reasoning with Cabrakkan, but he wouldn't listen. Olorus became enraged with Cabrakkan's ego, and he challenged him to a daji."

I took a deep breath in. "A fight," I said.

He looked into my eyes. "A fight to the death. Cabrakkan's strength was unrivaled. His skin could never be scraped, let alone sliced through. He was impossible to kill. But Cabrakkan underestimated Olorus. Olorus was smarter and more diligent than him by far. He found a way to use energy to slow Cabrakkan's movements down. Olorus also had a secret weapon. He'd created a special sword made from metal from a planet called Athias, which no one else could ever reach." He smiled. "The sword sliced through Cabrakkan's skin like no other instrument could have. Olorus beheaded Cabrakkan and was hoping for a change. Unfortunately, Cabrakkan was the lord of his people. The people of Cabrakkan's kingdom had more numbers and better weapons, and they did not want to change. They liked the old ways. They believed humans were lower than them, and they believed the same of the woman of their race. Cabrakkan's people didn't agree with Olorus, but they didn't attack right away.

"Olorus's wife died after giving birth to their daughter. Olorus found love again, but unfortunately, it wasn't in Argathia. When Olorus announced that his queen was a woman from the Aztecs, a human tribe, and that it was time for the kingdoms to integrate with the human race, many people became infuriated and revolted." He gave a pained sigh as if he was reliving the moment. "The son of Lord Cabrakkan, Sapien, the other people of Cabrakkan's tribe and some of Olorus's people found Lord Olorus and Lord Bakusura. They tied them down and chopped both their heads off with the sword Olorus had created. The two tribes left were those ruled by the sons of Cabrakkan and Sapien, who became the rulers of Inner Earth. Olorus's daughter was given a choice. She could marry one of the two kings and contribute to making a pure race, or she could submit herself to be killed. But the two kings weren't aware that Olorus's new queen had great power from her Aztec roots. Her tribe's blood had a special essence of magic given from a higher power, even higher than Cabrakkan. She cursed the people in Argathia, and she cursed her own people, sacrificing her soul and her whole tribe."

He paused again, gazing off into the distance. "They say that that night of revenge was so strong, so powerful, that it made the moon tremble." He looked me in the eye. "She murdered ninety percent of the people of Argathia, and the lords who lived there were never allowed to leave Argathia again."

My eyes became wide.

"It doesn't stop there," he continued. "She also cursed the blood of the original four kings, making it so that they could only sire a girl once every five thousand years, and those women would forever have the features of human Aztec women. She wanted to teach them a lesson that would remind them of what they'd done and avenge the death of Olorus."

I started thinking of what exactly this woman had gone through, losing the love of her life and sacrificing her own family and people for the sake of teaching the lords a lesson.

We were almost to the car, and I was about to ask a question when the handsome man stopped walking and took his black jacket off, wrapping me in it. The smell of him and the warmth made me feel dizzy.

"Rose," he said in such a way that I could not help but blush. "Olorus's daughter was named Alana. She was your mother."

CHAPTER 6

THE KISS

I felt like I'd been punched in the stomach. All I could do was stutter. "What?" I coughed, trying not to look like a fish gasping for air.

"She fled," he said with a sense of pride about him. "Your mother was strong. She covered her essence so the kings couldn't track her. But on your eighteenth birthday, your essence was found, and they have been tracking you ever since." He got very still.

"Are you … ?" I began to say, but he waved a hand, and my voice failed me. I tried to yell, but nothing happened. My eyes grew wide.

He gave me an apologetic look. "They found us already," he whispered under his breath. He pulled me close. "Please try not to breathe."

I began to feel heat course through my body. My cheeks turned red. How dare he do this to my voice? But before I could put up any kind of argument, something emerged from behind the car.

A huge black snake! No. I squinted harder. It had the head of a vicious dog, but it slithered on the ground like a snake. It had scaly black skin, and its eyes were metallic silver and slanted. It sniffed around the car, licking it with its tongue. Then it melted down to nothing more than a black puddle and slid through the cracks of the car, disappearing inside.

I could hear my heart pounding in my ears. Within seconds, the metallic black goop started coming back out of the car, and the liquid slowly started forming the dog-headed snake again. The creature began to slither off. Then something appeared in the tree behind the car. A golden sparkle seemed to gleam. I squinted but could not see what it was.

The man's grip tightened around me, and I could feel his hot breath on my neck. His body was slowly getting warmer.

I turned around to look at him. He was glaring at the golden shine with pure hatred. His eyes filled with anger and seemed to grow darker. He looked down at me.

I rubbed his arm up and down, giving him a look of concern. I'd never seen anyone look so angry and hurt. The more he looked at me, the more his eyes returned to the honey brown I recognized. He kept looking at me in silence until all the anger had gone. His eyes flooded with wonder and appreciation. "We have to move fast. This forcefield will only last for an hour max."

I'd heard what he'd said, but I was still concerned about why he'd looked so angry and hurt. "Why were you so mad?" I asked as we started walking quickly down the street.

"It's not important," he said dismissively, sounding ashamed for having let me see him so vulnerable.

I stopped walking. "Please don't do that."

He halted too, looking at me, shocked.

"Please don't shut yourself off from me."

He looked amazed. "Okay," he said. "That was someone who killed my friend. The things I want to do to him are beyond your imagination. But I vowed only to use my strength to protect, not to enact vengeance, even if it is well deserved."

I could feel his pain with every word. "I understand," I told him. "I felt that way about the driver who killed my mother. He died in the crash."

He shook his head. "Your mother did not die in a car accident."

My heart fluttered, and I looked up at him. "What?"

He continued. "She was murdered by one of the people of Argathia. The only thing that could have killed your mother is the sword from Athias."

A sharp pain pierced my chest.

"I will never lie to you, Rose."

All the anger I'd suppressed now came rushing to the surface.

"Rose?" he said, swiftly wrapping his arms around me.

I barely noticed him. I was violently shaking, and I started seeing colors again. This time, they were dark, gloomy colors, colors that heightened my anger.

"Rose, you have to calm down. Look at me." When I didn't listen, he lightly grabbed my face and forced it toward his. "I said look at me." His eyes were a flecked with metallic gold and sparks of blue.

The dark colors started bouncing off of him, and his eyes were all I could focus on. The anger started fading from my heart, and the colors dulled, becoming fuzzier.

After that, everything was a blur. I remembered waking up in a car, seeing his eyes again, feeling dizzy, and hearing him telling me, "We're going somewhere safe, a cabin."

When I awoke, I felt warm and calm. I was wrapped in a furry blanket, and for a moment, I felt completely at peace. Then everything came rushing back to me, and I jolted up and looked down. I was still in my long-sleeve shirt and jeans. I took a deep breath and tried to calm down. I then looked around the room. It was very homey-looking. A fireplace in the corner was lit, standing in contrast to a small window, which had frosted over and had not yet thawed. I noticed my bag on top of the dresser. I grabbed it and ran into the bathroom, which was attached to the room.

I didn't want to focus on my feelings. My emotions were mixed, and I didn't want to face them right now. I noticed the deep bathtub immediately. It was exactly what I needed. I filled the tub up to the brim and climbed in, soaking away my troubles. I let time drift away, staying there until the water turned cold. When I finally got out, I put on a fresh pair of pants and a black long-sleeve shirt. I ran my fingers through my hair, trying in vain to remove knots and tangles.

When I walked out, the energy of the handsome man's presence hit me instantly, even though he was just standing in the doorway. I looked up at him, and anger washed over me once more. "How dare you?" I spat.

He looked taken aback, but he didn't stay silent for long. "I'm sorry," he said. "But I had to make a decision. You were going to use powers you didn't know how to handle and—"

I cut him off. "You don't get to make decisions for me." I took a step closer, and it hit me within a second.

His aura felt dangerous. Fear struck me and made me hesitate. It was dark and strong, and something in me knew not to mess with this man. But I ignored all common sense and instinct. I stormed right up to him, stopping when I was only a few inches away. "I am fully capable of making my own decisions. This is my body and my mind. You should never take my choices from me."

He looked down as if ashamed of himself. "You're right." He stepped in close, and the dangerousness of aura disappeared, replaced by his body heat. "I am a fool. Please forgive me." His breath danced on my nose. "You are more than capable of figuring things out for yourself. I guess my protective nature took over. I'll try not to let it happen again. I promise." His eyes were wide and full of guilt.

My anger melted away as quickly as it had come. I looked into his eyes and felt an emotion I had never felt before. Was it happiness or gratitude? No, it was deeper than that. Was it love? "Well, thank you," I said more shortly than I meant to, taking a step back.

He looked mesmerized by me.

I blushed and looked down at the floor. It was quiet for a minute. All I could hear was the fire crackling, and all I could feel was the heat between us, which far outperformed the warmth of the flame.

"You are too beautiful for this universe," he said quietly as he started to turn away. "We will be leaving soon, and before long, we will be in Argathia. We will be walking quite some distance. I can only cover so much of your essence, and in a car, it's much harder."

As we walked out of the front door, the smell of earth and wood hit my nose. "Where are we?" I asked, looking around at all the greenery. There had to be thousands of dark green trees, ranging from twenty to forty feet in height. Even though the sun was out, it was quite chilly. I wrapped my hooded poncho around me and tied it at my neck.

"Ireland," he said.

I huffed. "Great. I should fit right in here with my jet-black hair."

He shot me a smile. "They would be blessed to have you as one of their own, but sadly, you are already taken," he said, claiming me for himself. His eyes bore into mine, waiting for my reaction.

Something in me jumped as I felt that dangerous yet mesmerizing aura again, drawing me in, daring me to taste it. I folded and tried to change the subject. "You mentioned powers earlier. What did you mean?"

He became serious. "As I mentioned before, we are a different species. Everyone has different gifts. Your mother could heal, and I believe that when she used a lot of her essence or got mad, she could move things with her mind." He coughed. "Or make things explode. I believe she dabbled in magic as well. Not everyone can do magic. Only certain bloodlines are capable of containing that kind of energy."

I listened quietly, nodding my head every so often to show that I understood.

"The potion Lou gave you activated all your essence and power at once," he told me. "A lot of people get very sick from it because it heightens your essence." He paused. "Some have even died, but I think he was just trying to make sure you were the real deal. Your mother did an amazing job hiding your scent and powers. It's probably going to be hard for you to use them when you figure them out."

I sighed. Of course, nothing would be easy. Of course, I couldn't have a normal life, going to college and becoming someone my mother would have been proud of. Then again, had I even known my mother? I'd thought she was an archeologist, but it now turned out that she'd been from a whole different species and a whole other place. I smiled. Actually, that did sound like her. She'd always been so stubborn and fierce; that was why I loved her. Besides, had I ever really felt like I was living to be who I truly was? I'd never felt connected, and now I knew why. "How are things in Argathia now?" I asked.

The man sighed. "To be honest, I don't know. I've stayed away as much as possible, but if I had to guess, probably the same. They need change, Rose. Argathia is beautiful. It would be a great place for a new kingdom, but who is willing to fight for that change?" He looked at me meaningfully.

Something stirred in my chest. The wind blew my hair in front of my face, and I felt something I'd never felt before: purpose.

We walked for another thirty minutes. "Have you even been here before?" I asked eventually.

"There is no place on Earth I haven't been," he said. "This is one of my favorite places. Luckily for me, it happens to be where one of the entrances to Argathia lies." He continued to talk about the history of Ireland and what made it so beautiful.

I stared unashamedly, entranced by every movement of his face. The way his eyes crinkled at the sides when he spoke about the beauty of Ireland. The way one piece of hair kept falling in front of his beautiful eyes. Suddenly, I stopped walking, and he stopped talking, turning to find out why. I reached over and tucked the strand of hair that kept falling behind his ear.

His eyes became pools of emotion, and he touched my hand softly as I brought it down to my waist. He looked at me, and I looked up at him. It was almost sunset, and hues of red and orange danced through the trees, landing on his face.

I realized something. "What is your name?" I asked in a soft voice. I needed to know it. I needed to know who he was, the man who'd stolen my heart in days, the man whose aura was intoxicating, the man who'd saved me not only from evil but from my own mind.

He laughed. "Ah, what is a name? Would a rose by any other name not smell as sweet?" Then he became serious. "My name is Damien."

I nodded. Then I noticed light flickering across Damien's face. I thought I was seeing colors again, but when I looked closer, I saw that it was a firefly. I saw another, then another, then another. Soon, there were hundreds of fireflies soaring around us.

Damien's face lit up, his eyes sparkling in awe. "This is one of my favorite places at this time of year. It's where the fireflies come to nest and dance."

It was like I was in a dream that I never wanted to wake up from. I spun around, smiling like a kid dancing in the rain for the first time. I'd never seen something so beautiful in all my life. Then I stopped spinning right in front of him.

Damien's eyes were locked on my lips. "Rose, may I kiss you?"

The dangerous aura around him grew and mixed with desire. I felt like I was being sucked in, but I didn't care. I needed to know what his lips would feel like on mine. "Yes."

The fireflies seemed to be motionless now. The air was still, and his movements were slow. He tucked my hair behind my ears and slowly leaned in.

When our lips finally met, it felt like I was flying. My lips were swimming in pools of soft liquid. I was in pure bliss.

After the first kiss, he pulled back, looking as happy as I felt.

I wanted more. I slowly moved in to kiss him again, and he obliged, this time grabbing my waist tighter and pulling me closer. He wanted this kiss just as badly as I did.

He pulled back too soon.

"Why?" I breathed, my eyes still closed, my lips still tingling.

He leaned his back against a tree and clenched his jaw. "Rose, there's more you need to know about me and about yourself."

I was confused. I raised an eyebrow questioningly.

"My God, you are beautiful," he said.

I smiled. "Is that what I needed to know?"

He was breathing more evenly now. He shook his head. "No, I just wanted to tell you how I felt." He paused. "To start with, I want you to know that where I come from, we take what we want. We do not ask because we are stronger and more vicious than anything on this Earth. And most things beyond it." He looked at me. "There are different types of people who live in Argathia. I told you that earlier. But we all have one thing in common. We feed off the essence of life."

I stumbled back. "What?"

He took a step forward from the tree, now completely composed. "Everything has an essence. Plants, animals, humans. We can survive off plant essence, but there are people who take it from humans, and sometimes, people can't control themselves. Like you and I."

I felt myself reeling. I tried to process what he was saying. "I don't understand."

"We just fed off each other's essences, Rose. One of the reasons why Argathians breed with each other is because we can kill humans by draining them of their energy and essence. It's hard. Once you get a taste, it can feel very good, especially if there are strong emotions tied to it." He paused, looking at me, waiting for a reaction.

"Is that a bad thing? I mean, can it hurt us?" I asked.

He started walking closer to me. "No, but the weaker one of the two will soon begin to feel tired and weak, while the stronger will be filled with strength and energy." He was face to face with me again, looking me up and down, checking to see if I was hurt. "I want you to know that I respect you. I will always be honest with you."

I nodded, disappointed that, in the absence of his kiss, the high feeling was slipping away.

"I'm in love with you," he told me. The air grew still. He looked down at me. "I have never felt like this before, but I've read about it, and I've seen it in other people. I know that I am completely in love with you." He chuckled in disbelief. "I have been watching you. I have seen how you care for others before yourself, your fervor for what's right, your energy, your beauty, the fight in your spirit." He brought his eyes slowly to mine. "Your beauty is unmatched."

I turned my head slightly to the side.

He put his hand softly under my chin and turned it upwards. His voice was soft and gentle. "I understand if—"

"I'm in love with you too." I blurted the words out faster than my mind could process. And I knew in my heart that they were true.

This time, he didn't ask to kiss me. He just did. Slowly, passionately, with emotion in every movement. After what felt like a mere second of bliss, he grabbed my hand. "We're here," he stated. He smiled and took out a knife. "Only Argathians can open the portal." He drew a symbol in the dirt and cut his hand, spilling blood onto the symbol. The ground began sinking in. He grabbed my waist and whispered in my ear, "Hold on tight."

It felt like being sucked into a hole of nothingness. Then, suddenly, we were floating gently atop green and golden grass. Damien's arm was still firmly wrapped around my waist.

My eyes adjusted to the light. The sun shone brightly, giving everything a golden hue. The trees stood tall in shades of green I had never even seen before. Rivers of pink and blue spread as far as I could see, and in the distance, I could see gold buildings and one huge golden estate. I gasped.

"Beautiful, isn't it?" Damien said.

I took a step forward. "Yes," I sputtered out.

A huge butterfly-looking creature flew by, but it wasn't like any butterfly I knew of. It had to be at least three feet wide, and it had human-looking eyes. It stopped right in front of me and blinked. I blinked back, and we stared at each other for thirty seconds.

"Should I be jealous?" Damien laughed. "I think he likes you."

I was in a daze. "What was that?" I asked as the butterfly flew away.

"One of King Cabrakkan's creations, I'm sure."

"What do you mean by creations?" I continued looking around, taking in the beauty of this world.

"King Cabrakkan has the power to create life from what already exists. He can alter appearance."

I nodded.

"Sapien has the gift of taking life," Damien continued.

I froze.

"He can take it quickly, and you won't even notice." He stepped in front of me. "I will not let anything happen to you, Rose." His eyes grew fierce and dangerous. "You have come here to make a choice. You can choose to stay here with your people and try to change things to your liking, or you can go back to Earth. Either way, I am here to protect and guide you." He smiled. "Besides, it's me you should be worried about." He pulled me close. "I'm more dangerous than both of them."

"Please," I said. "I could take you."

He laughed loudly. "Oh, yeah? Is that a challenge, flower?" Before I could even make a move, he grabbed my waist and pinned me to the ground, but he made sure my head touched it softly. His body pressed against mine. "Good thing you're smart. Strength is not in your favor."

I looked up, wide-eyed. "Who is that?"

He quickly released me, and as he tried to stumble to his feet, I stuck out my foot and tripped him, making him tumble back down to the ground.

"Good thing you're not very smart," I said as I began to get up and brush myself off.

He laughed. "Well, the rose has thorns after all." But his laughter didn't last. Suddenly, he stopped, and in the blink of an eye, he was in front of me. "How did they find us already?"

Five tiger-headed golden hawks that had to be at least ten feet long soared through the sky. Each one was ridden by a soldier dressed in gold. They landed right in front of us, the force creating a wind that blew my hair around my face.

Only the middle soldier got off his bird-like creature. He immediately dropped to one knee. "Lady Rose, I am here to escort you to the king." He banged his chest three times with his fist and bowed his head.

I looked at Damien. "Yes, we will go," I said, wanting to explore this new land.

Damien looked worried. "I was going to take you to the other kingdom first …"

I looked at the beauty all around me and made up my mind. "No, let's go to this one."

He nodded, but I could tell that he wasn't happy.

They saddled the creature up for me to sit, and Damien, who refused a saddle, sat behind me. The bird took off, sending a jolt through my body. I'd never felt so awake and free. The wind rushed through my hair, and the golden sun warmed my face. I closed my eyes and took in this moment of freedom. I felt untouchable. When I opened my eyes and looked down, it was like I was floating over a painting. The golden kingdom was huge. Creatures I had never seen before marched along the streets, walking through the crowds. Some were giants, standing over nine feet tall. Others had tails, and still more had tentacles. They shopped and socialized as if this were the norm. We flew above them all and soon landed behind a large golden castle.

As we walked up to the castle, I noticed that everything was made of gears of different shapes and sizes, all constantly turning. This building was truly a masterpiece. The five guards walked in front of me, and Damien walked behind me as we climbed the staircase that led up to the castle doors.

The doors opened slowly, and out walked a ten-foot-tall jolly king, who wore a crown studded with jewels I didn't recognize and an extravagant golden robe. He had a beaming smile, rosy cheeks, and a stomach that jiggled when he walked. He laughed loudly. "Welcome, Rose."

The guards dropped to their knees and stayed there.

He opened his arms wide. "Welcome to my kingdom."

Horns sounded, and out walked a woman no taller than five foot. She had icy blue skin and eyes to match. Her white hair shone in the light, and a crown too big for her head sat atop her slicked-back bun. She stood next to the king, not making eye contact with me.

The horn sounded again, and three tall men walked out. The first was slender and had white hair and blue eyes. He was staring daggers at me as if I were a piece of meat.

Damien put his hand on my back, and I heard a low growl come from his throat.

The second man had red hair and golden-brown eyes. He didn't really seem to want to be there.

And the last of the men, I knew. It was Lou. He emerged wearing golden clothing and a charming smile. He winked at me. "Come join us for dinner," he said. "Let us give you a proper Luthernian welcome."

CHAPTER 7

ARGATHIA

I walked behind the king and his wife, the three sons walking before the queen.

"I'm sure you have many questions," the king yelled to me, his voice sounding jovial. "I will be glad to answer them all after we eat. I'm sure you're famished from your travels. The guards will take you to your quarters. It's going to be lovely having you here," he said in a soothing tone.

As we reached the stairs, I noticed that they were moving of their own accord. The guard stepped on one step and asked me to join him. Damien followed right behind me, earning a look of annoyance from the guard. But Damien was focused on me; I could feel his gaze.

"Quarter five, room one," the guard said. He tapped on the server twice with his staff. The stairs came to life, moving smoothly upward, higher and higher.

Damien put his hand on the small of my back to balance me.

When we stopped in front of the door, the staircase melted into the ground. "Your quarters, Madame Rose," the guard said. "I'll stand out here until you're ready to go." He tapped the staff twice and stood without moving, not even blinking.

As I stood at the door, I was mesmerized by its beauty. It was gold, and the shapes of small lions and eagles were carved into it. I looked closer, and I noticed that they were moving slowly, changing their shapes and positions. I took a step forward to take a closer look, but the door opened. Instantly, the lions and eagles left my mind. I was consumed by the extravagance of the room. The room was white and gold with hues of rose pink splattered throughout it. None of the furniture touched the floor. Instead, it floated in midair. The couch was golden and had a satin sheen, and the tables were gold, covered in plaques that bore the same designs of lions and eagles running and shifting. As I walked further in, I became more and more enraptured by the room. There was a ten-foot-tall window with real rosebushes dancing around its frame, and there were tulips by the large fireplace. I walked into the bedroom, where a bed the size of my room back at home floated above the ground, a gold satin blanket draping off of it.

I almost forgot where I was until I felt electric energy behind me. Damien whispered in my ear, "Beautiful, isn't it?"

"It's the most beautiful thing I've ever seen," I breathed.

He laughed. "This is nothing compared to you." He started walking around, looking up and down, seeming unimpressed. "Remember, Rose, all that glitters isn't gold." He picked up a piece of the golden drape and dropped it.

"I take it gold isn't your favorite color," I said.

He smiled and returned to me, running a hand through my long black hair. "No, I'm more of a black kind of guy." He took a piece of hair and tucked it behind my ear. "How are you feeling?" he asked.

I sat on the bed. "I'm feeling good," I told him honestly. "A little overwhelmed. I'm just trying to take everything in. So, this king … creates things?"

Damien sat down next to me. "Yes, his father Cabrakkan had the same power and more. Of course, the king must have a muse, but he can create what he wants and how he wants it."

I sighed wistfully. "Tell me more about the king and his kingdom. He seems so happy. He's nothing like the king I envisioned trying to force my mother to marry."

Damien sighed too. "I want you to form your own opinion about the people you meet here. After all, it's your decision if you want to stay."

I nodded. “So, where’s the other king?” I asked.

“The kingdoms are separate,” Damien answered. “The other king is about five hours from here. His kingdom is very different from this one.” He looked down. “Remember, this king is the creator of life, but the other king is the creator of death.”

Before I could ask anything more, I heard a knock on the door. I walked to the door and opened it.

A sweet lady stood on the other side. She was about four feet tall and very round. She had stark-white hair and looked to be at least seventy-four years old. She wore large gold-framed glasses, and she had a warm grandmotherly smile. “Hello, miss,” she squeaked. “I’m here to take your measurements and get you ready for lunch.”

My eyes widened. “Excuse me?” I demanded.

She fiddled with her glasses. “Yes, we’re going to get you out of those threads and into something more fitting.”

My face darkened.

The lady smiled, hardly seeming to notice my displeasure. “If it makes you feel better, I’ll let you pick the color.” One of her old, wrinkled eyes gave me a wink.

Damien came up behind me and gently moved my hair from my neck. “When in Rome, am I right?” he whispered in my ear. “I would love to see what you look like out of your jeans and shirt, though you do look ravishing already.”

I felt chills creep down my spine, my heart fluttered, and warmth tingled through my body.

The old woman gave Damien a disapproving look. "Exit," she told him snippily.

Damien put his hands up as if pleading innocence. "I won't be far," he said, walking out.

When the door shut behind him, the woman huffed and rubbed her hands together. "Now, watch me create a masterpiece." She waddled back to the door, getting something out of her bag. It was then I noticed that her bottom half looked just like the bottom half of a duck. She had a fluffy duck tail and short webbed feet. She took a small golden ball out and pressed its top. Two sides sprung open and started moving all around me.

I quickly turned my head.

"Uh-uh!" she said. "Don't move, or we're going to have to do it all over again."

I stood still, trying not to flinch as it fluttered faster and faster, swirling all around my hips and my neck. Then it abruptly stopped and moved back to her, falling into her hand.

"Now, what is your favorite color?" she said with the air of someone who was doing me a favor.

I smiled. "Black," I responded.

Her whole face drooped. "Black," she repeated in a monotone voice.

I smiled bigger. "Yep."

She sighed and rubbed her temples. "Well, this will definitely give me a challenge." She took the golden ball and pressed it so hastily that I couldn't tell what exactly she was pressing.

The ball jumped to life again and slowly started creating an image of the top of a shoulder, then another shoulder. The image started to turn black, and I realized it was a dress. I watched in astonishment. In the blink of an eye, the ball was finished. The result was a long-sleeve black dress with sparkles of gold around its deep collar and middle, forming a golden belt. It looked like something out of a dream. I walked up to it, touching it lightly.

The woman smiled. "I had to add *some* gold to it," she explained. "You don't want the king to fire me, do you?"

"No," I said. "It's beautiful."

She smiled contentedly. "I do pride myself on my work. All right. Now get dressed, and for goodness' sake, let me do your hair."

I went into the bathroom and took a shower, then put on the dress and let the woman do my hair. As she brushed it into place, I asked her what her name was.

She looked taken aback. "I don't have a name," she told me.

"What do you mean?" I asked, confused.

She waddled backwards. "I was never given a name by the king."

I was getting upset. "What do you mean?" I asked, feeling frustrated. "What did your mother and father call you?"

Her face clouded with confusion. "What's a mother or father? The king is my creator, and I do his will. That is all I know."

I took a deep breath and steadied myself against this revelation. "Well, you remind me of my friend's grandmother, and her name was Dorothy," I told the woman. "I'm going to call you Dorothy."

She repeated the name slowly. "Dorothy. I like it." Moments later, she heard a buzz coming from her pocket. "I'm being called. I must go." She took one last look at me before walking out. She smiled widely. "I think you are my greatest masterpiece yet," she told me earnestly. Then she waddled off.

As she walked away, I took a quick glance in the mirror. I was startled. I looked just like my mother. Half of my hair was curled into a beautiful bun, the other half twisting down my shoulders. I squinted my eyes to look harder at the dress, but as I did, I saw something move on the sink. My eyes shot over to it.

It was a bottle of what looked like perfume. It started to float upward and tried to spritz me. I ducked and looked around madly, trying to see if I was crazy, but sure enough, it tried to spritz me again. I dodged it once, taking a step back, but it persisted. We kept at this battle for a minute before I slapped it down on the floor and huffed in victory as I moved a piece of hair out of my eyes.

Then I turned around slowly and saw him: the man of my dreams. His head was tilted down a bit, but his eyes locked on me, filled with hunger and desire. His dangerous aura surrounded him. He smiled and pointed behind me.

The perfume was back in full force, spraying all around me. I fluttered my hands uselessly.

Damien barely kept the amusement out of his voice. “No, thank you,” he told the bottle firmly.

The bottle jolted to a halt and settled back on the counter, lifeless.

Damien stepped in closer, swooping down on me like a hawk on its prey. “We have to work on those combat skills.”

I smiled. “Knocked you off your feet.”

He kissed my hand softly. “More than you know.”

I blushed deeply.

“You look breathtaking,” he said as we started walking out the door.

It was weird. Even though I was in a whole other world, dressed in clothes unlike anything I'd ever worn,

I felt right at home when he was next to me. "You're too kind," I said, looking down.

The guard was still outside the door, standing so still that he barely looked real. Upon my approach, he turned toward me, his eyes coming to life. "Step ahead, Madame Rose."

Damien and I stepped on the stairs, the guard behind us. He took his staff and hit the floor twice, and the stairs began to shift again. It was quite a sight to see all the gilded gears moving in the walls as if they had an essence of their own. We rose until we reached the top. The stairs melted into the floor, and I looked around. The room was empty. All I could see were the walls, which were covered in golden flakes, and the ceiling, which was see-through, revealing the beautiful blue sky.

Suddenly, I heard two taps from the guard, and a light breeze hit my face and whipped my hair. The room came to life. There was a grand table filled with the most delicious foods I'd ever seen. I spotted the king, who was laughing and holding his belly. His wife sat gracefully by his side. Two of their sons sat next to their mother.

Lou was next to his father on the right. "Welcome," he said with a smile.

Damien had a concerned look on his face.

"Madame, to your right. Gentleman, to your left," the guard instructed.

Damien didn't seem to want to move. "You know, we can go back home whenever you like," he said in a low voice.

I touched his hand lightly. "Thank you, but let's enjoy this feast." I was famished, and the food looked amazing.

Damien sat next to the two brothers grudgingly, and I sat next to Lou.

Lou shot Damien a harsh glare. Then he turned his attention to me. "Rose, welcome to my kingdom. Please fill your stomach with the delicacies of my land."

There were mint-green puff balls and yellow loaves of bread. It all smelled like my favorite bakery. I filled my plate with a generous helping and began to eat.

"Why, hello, princess," Lou said with a smile. "Fancy meeting you here."

I rolled my eyes. "You drugged me, Lou, if that's even your real name."

He reeled back. "I would never! I was preparing you." He took a bite of bread. "And yes, my name is Lou."

"What do you mean preparing me, huh?" I demanded. "Preparing me for you to kidnap me?" I took a bite of my bread as well, and I saw Damien watching us out the corner of my eye. His plate was empty, I noticed.

"You think you could have made it to Argathia without me?" Lou asked. "Your essence had to be purified to its original state."

I took a sip of my drink. "Okay, but who gave you the right to do that?"

Lou sighed and looked at me sorrowfully. "There are orders even I have no choice but to follow."

The king hit his staff on the ground, and everyone looked at him, silence falling. He cleared his throat and began to speak. "Rose, I am sure you have many questions. Let us discuss them." He let go of his staff, and it hung perfectly still in midair.

Everyone around me grew quiet, and I felt the king's stare, along with everybody else's, burning through my forehead. All the attention on me was making me anxious, and the questions that had been running through my mind earlier suddenly went blank. I forced out the only thing I could think of. "So, you create things?"

The king repeated what I'd said and laughed heartily. As his laugh settled, he looked into my eyes and said, "I do so much more than create things. I create worlds. I create life. I create cities." He straightened his posture and started telling me about all the things he'd created, clearly very proud. "So, Rose, what do you think about my creations?"

I could feel the air in the room get a little staler, though I didn't know why. "I think your home and city are beautiful," I said lowly.

The king didn't look as smiley as before. "No, I mean my creations. My soldiers, my servants, the creatures in my city. My creations. What do you think?"

Something inside me burned. I didn't like how he spoke about the people in his city as if they were objects. I cleared my throat. "I think that the people you created are beautiful and should be treated as such."

The king touched the stone on the top of his staff.

I was beginning to suspect that a dangerous burst of anger was coming. I gulped.

Then the king smiled broadly. "Did you like the food?"

I thought that was an odd question to ask given what we were talking about, but maybe he was trying to lift the mood. I took another sip of my drink. "Yes, I thought it was lovely."

I'd barely finished before he shot me another question. "How do you feel?" he asked curiously.

I hadn't really been paying attention until he mentioned it, but I noticed it now. I felt high and strong, as though I could breathe clearly for the first time. "I guess I feel better than normal," I said, forcing a smile.

"Do you know, Rose, that our people are more valuable and more important than any people in this universe?" the king said. "Do you know that there was a time when my people ruled almost every planet in this universe? We were strong, unstoppable. We were unfazed by emotion and compassion, for those are such weak qualities."

The more he spoke, the more the anger began to build up in my chest.

"Our people thrived off the weak, and the women stayed in their place and supported the men. The men did what was needed to make sure our race reigned supreme. One thing that makes us stronger, invincible, even, is sucking in the essence of life itself."

I was beginning to feel confused, frustrated, and angry. What was going on?

"The food that you're eating is mixed with human essence," the king continued. "That's why you feel so strong." He looked away from his staff and stared deep into my eyes.

"How dare you?" I spat, shaking with anger, fear, and anticipation.

The king laughed. "How dare I?" his voice boomed.

I tried to stand up, but it felt like something heavy was on top of my body. I couldn't move. I couldn't even speak.

"Sit down when you are in the presence of a king, girl," he said with a rumble in his throat. "I've been watching you ever since you came here. I've been studying your essence and spirit. You are weak," he said, disgust in his voice. "All women are weak, but you have compassion and empathy for people and creatures that are beneath you, which makes you the weakest of all. The only thing they are good for is to be conquered. Look at them," he said. "They are weak, feeble, breakable. They are prey."

Anger coursed through me. I glared at him, and the table I was leaning on started shaking under my grip.

"Oh, you look just like your mother," the king said. "That's too bad."

I looked around and realized something terrible. Everybody was frozen. Nobody could talk. Nobody could even move. I looked at Damien. There was a golden shield around him, and I could see his neck muscles straining, his energy slowly seeping through whatever was keeping him immobile. That aura of danger was just waiting to attack. His eyes were dark, looking straight at the king.

"One thing you will never have to worry about is me hiding things from you," the king said in a calmer tone. He started walking toward me, coming close enough that I could feel his breath on my skin. "Unlike your lover over there," he whispered in my ear, standing behind me. "You might know him as Damien, which is partly true. It was almost hard for me to see who he truly was. But you, my dear girl, are looking at the reincarnation of Bakusura."

My chest fell for a second, and I looked at Damien, searching his eyes for the truth.

He returned my gaze, looking as if he wished he could have told me himself.

"See, girl?" said the king. "He thinks he's the only one who can switch his essence out of his body, but he's not the only one who knows the ritual." Now he was eyeing Damien. "The day of the daji, I switched souls with my eldest son." He laughed deeply.

The gold shield around Damien started to crack, but the king hit his rod on the floor, and in an instant, Damien was sucked underground. I looked frantically to Lou for help, but he was frozen as well. I tried to run, but I still couldn't move. I fought to harness my anger, but before I could, I felt the ground slip beneath me, and I got sucked through the ground and into a black hole.

When I awoke, I was in a beautiful golden room. The bed was so comfortable and soft that I felt as if I was sleeping on a cloud. Had it all been a dream? I sat up, all the memories from the dinner rushing back. I ran to the door, but there was no door handle. I began to panic. I banged on the door and searched, feeling around to see if there was a button or something I could push. There was nothing. I ran to the window, which was barred up with gold, and looked down. I had to be at least fifty stories high. I wasn't sleeping. This wasn't a dream. My anxiety took over, sending me spiraling. It was real, all of it, and I was trapped inside this room.

CHAPTER 8

TRAPPED

I kicked the door as hard as I could, then paced around the room like a hamster stuck in a cage, searching for an exit. When my search was unsuccessful, I returned to kicking and punching the door, yelling profanities at the top of my lungs. Damien's face appeared in my head. Where was he? Was he okay? Was he gone? Why was this happening?

I rested my back against the door and slid down it slowly, my eyes welling up with tears.

"Rose," came a familiar raspy voice. Lou.

I looked around, but I couldn't see him. I noticed something on the desk and rushed over to it. Floating in midair was a seven-inch-tall version of Lou, see-through and flickering with specks of gold.

"How could you do this to me?" I asked pleadingly.

Lou whispered, "It wasn't supposed to be like this. My father does whatever he pleases whenever he pleases."

Anger stirred up in me. "You just let him," I yelled, my face reddening.

Lou shushed me. "Please stop yelling. I could get in big trouble for talking to you like this."

Anger still bubbling inside me, I forced out my next question through gritted teeth. "How could you let him trap me? How can you let him do what he does to humans?"

Lou just shook his head. "Rose, it is so much worse than you know, but I have no choice. I am bound to him. I am bound to this place. I can only do what he wishes."

"Lies," I hissed. "You choose to do this. You could fight this, fight him. I know he's your father, but he's wrong. Get me out of here, and I'll help you. We'll find a way. We'll find Damien, and we'll fight the king together."

Lou looked to the side. "Rose, Damien isn't all you know him to be. Besides, he's probably dead by now."

My heart felt like it had been ripped out of my chest. I couldn't breathe, and my vision blurred with tears. I could barely see Lou.

Lou began to speak again, but suddenly, a look of terror came over him, and his tiny figure disappeared.

Before I could say his name, I heard the king's voice and felt his aura. It was different than before. It hit my chest like a ton of bricks. It was dark and overpowering, making me want to go and hide under the covers. "Apparently, you can't even trust your own sons anymore," he said calmly, giving a malicious chuckle.

Even with the power radiating from him, my anger took over, doing away with my inhibitions. I ran toward him. "You!" I screamed. That was all I could get out before something struck my stomach, knocking the air out of me.

The king was five feet away, but he'd slammed some kind of invisible shield into my stomach. He pointed his staff at me, rage filling his eyes. He took his staff and swiped it sharply, and I flew across the room, my back hitting the wall, where I slid down to the ground, still fighting to catch my breath and trying not to pass out. "You, Rose, will learn your place very quickly," the king told me coldly. "Next time, I will break every bone in your body."

I tried to speak, but I couldn't form the words.

The king sighed. "Don't bother fighting or trying to talk. One of your ribs is broken. Just listen."

I grunted in pain.

"Rose, you must understand the way the universe works," he told me as if explaining something very simple to a child. "The strong, powerful, and unemotional survive and conquer." He looked at me with distaste in his eyes. "The weak, meek, and compassionate die and are conquered. They are good for nothing but to be servants to the elite" He took a step closer to me. "That is what the universe runs on: power. Your mother was a fool. All that power wasted! Don't be like her."

I shot him a look of hatred and spite. Through my gritted teeth, I wheezed out, "Don't you ever talk—"

But before I could finish, the king's humongous face was in mine, his golden eyes full of anger. He grabbed my jaw and jerked it sharply, making it crack. "I told you to know your place, girl. You don't know what you're dealing with." His voice was quiet and filled with venom.

A moment later, I reeled back in horror. Half of the king's face began to peel off, revealing his true face, not that of a jolly, happy king but a face of true evil power. His skin was comprised of black boils. His teeth were long and pointy, overlapping with each other. His eyes were long and wide, a shade of gold I'd never seen before. The sight of him made my heart race with fear. He smiled with both sides of his face. "This is true power, Rose. Terrifying, isn't it? Makes it so you can barely move or breathe." He came in closer, and I tried to turn my head, but his hand was wrapped around my neck, holding it in place. He stuck out his long, slender tongue, forked like a snake's, and licked my face. "You taste just like your mother," he said in a sickening tone. He growled and slowly began to rise. "I hope you're not as stubborn as she was." He restored his human mask and looked down at me.

My ribs were screaming in pain, and my jaw hurt even worse, but all I could think about was Damien. Was he still alive? What had the king done to him? My vision grew hazy. "Damien," I whispered. "Damien."

The king laughed. "Oh, Damien. Yes. I see you like a weak man, just like your mother." He walked over to sit in the chair by the desk, using his staff to make it bigger and wider so he could fit comfortably. "Do you know how long I have been waiting for this revenge?" Happiness glinted in his eyes. "Bakusura split from me once, but I will not let it happen again."

Confusion raced through my mind, and I furrowed my eyebrows.

"Oh, yes, Rose. Your Damien is the original Bakusura." The king laughed heartily. "Although he doesn't live up to his name anymore. His strength and essence have worn off. Time has not been kind to him. He has been weakened by you humans and by not using human essence. That's why he got beheaded the first time." He created a huge golden cup and poured himself a drink.

I lay unmoving on the floor beneath him, withered, broken, and in pain.

"And that's why he will get beheaded this time," the king continued. "I'm letting my dogs chew for a bit first, torture him some. I will put his head in my trophy room."

Hot tears streamed down my face, not from the pain but from my heart being broken, from imaging Damien, the only man I'd ever loved, being tortured.

"The audacity of him to think I would ever let him have you, my greatest trophy of all," said the king. "I will use you to breed a pure bloodline for my eldest son. Your joint power will create superb children." He looked off to the left as if talking to himself. "I'm excited to see what powers you possess." His eyes locked on me. "You are weak and feeble, but your essence is strong, like your mother's. It's almost hard for me to resist taking you for my own." He growled hungrily, then sighed. "But alas, I promised you to my eldest. Lou wasn't too happy about that, but he is not as strong as his brother, and I want the best in my bloodline. He will have to pay for contacting you without my permission. You see, I control everything here, and when there is something out of order, it's up to me to either kill or punish it." He laughed. "Like when my creation told me you gave it a name. Dorothy." He laughed again. "That was when I knew you were like your mother, stupid and naïve, looking at everything like it's equal. Don't worry, Rose. I will change that mindset quickly. I will beat it out of you." He rose and moved closer to me, then stopped. "The punishment for my creations stepping out of line is death, so you will not have a seamstress anymore." He smirked upon seeing tears stream down my face. "But death won't stop there for the people you have had compassion for. All your precious friends at that college. Madeline, Caroline, your fake father, your closest friend, Tyler … They will all die because of your love and compassion. And lastly, I will kill those weak emotions in you."

I had caused so much death, so much pain. It wasn't fair. It wasn't right. I tried to get up, but I couldn't.

The king smiled once more. "Don't worry. I will see you soon, hopefully in better shape. Make sure you get plenty of rest. We want our bloodline to be the strongest and best it can be, so do as you're told. I don't want to have to hurt the body that's going to carry my future heirs." He pointed his staff at me and began to chant in a language I'd never heard before. "Mushor blakina polari!"

Gold flakes began to dance around me, first at my jaw, then at my stomach. They slowly began to take the pain away.

"Your ribs and jaw will be fixed by tomorrow morning," the king told me. "When I leave this room, you will sleep. When you wake, you will dress in the clothes laid out for you, and you will meet your future husband." He smiled, showing another glimpse of his true face. Then he tapped his staff twice on the floor, and in a huge swirl of gold, he disappeared.

I lay there, feeling pain, depression, and anguish wash over me in waves. I stared up at the golden ceiling, praying that this was all a dream. Then I fell into a deep sleep.

The next morning, I woke to the chirping of a bird. My eyes opened slowly, and the first thing I saw was the ugly gold ceiling again. I shut my eyes tightly, refusing to believe that this was real. I opened them once more, blinking into the gold. Tears rolled down my cheeks. I listened to the bird, its chirping growing louder. I stood up gingerly and walked over to the small barred window. I noticed that my ribs felt better, but my jaw still ached.

The bird was tiny, no taller than five inches. It was a beautiful shade of blue. As I walked closer, it looked petrified and began to shake, chirping louder and louder. My tears felt cold as they dried on my cheeks. The bird's foot was trapped in a small crack in the window ledge. I tried to pull it out gently, but it was well and truly stuck. The bird chirped frantically and began thrashing around. I tried to still it, to calm it, but it was no use. I heard a quiet snap as the bird's leg broke. Its chest moved up and down rapidly, and I could tell it was in pain.

"I'm so sorry," I whispered as I scooped the bird in my hand and lightly petted its head. Here I was, messing things up again. Why hadn't I listened to Damien when he'd urged me to let us leave? I looked around. "I'm so sorry you're trapped with me," I told the bird. "I wish I could heal your leg."

I wanted to do something right. I wanted to fix something. I put my head down in pity. Suddenly, the bird's chirping stopped, and gold flakes like the ones the king had used on me started dancing around the little bird's leg. I gasped and almost dropped it, but I steadied myself, continuing to hold the bird until it flew out of my hand. It soared around me, then zipped out the window. I looked down at my hands, watching two or three remaining flakes fade from my palms. How was it possible? Maybe some of the king's spell was still having an effect on me.

As I looked down, I took in the now tattered dress Dorothy had made for me. I teared up thinking about her. I needed to change and regroup. I needed to plan my escape.

I drew myself a scorching hot bath in the regal golden tub and dipped my head under the water, holding my breath until I could no longer think.

After hours of stewing in the hot water, I finally got out, and hanging in the bathroom was a long golden gown covered with gold glitter and featuring a gold lion in the middle. I scoffed. "I'd rather die than be part of your abomination of a court."

I looked at myself in the mirror, and my reflection smiled back at me. Was I losing my mind? No, I was gaining clarity. My soulmate was dead, I'd gotten the people I loved killed, and I was trapped in this room, mere weeks, maybe even days, ahead of being forced to carry the spawn of these evil creatures. I knew what I had to do. I had to go out fighting, just as my mother would have. I punched the glass mirror and watched blood drip down my knuckles. I took the biggest piece of glass and cut the dress to above my knees. I tore the sleeves off and ripped the lion medallion away from the fabric, throwing it on the ground. Blood splattered the dress where the lion had been. I then took the piece of glass and smiled for a second. Tyler would be so proud—no hairspray this time. I put the dress on, blood all over it, and went to sit in the desk chair, waiting for my final fight with the shard of mirror glass in my hand.

He came quicker than I'd expected. I couldn't have been waiting for more than an hour. He walked through the door swiftly, almost as if gliding on the air. He looked different. Brown hair had replaced white, and he had bright green eyes. He looked like something out of a magazine. He was clothed in black and gold and smiled widely when he came in. He spun around, watching me look at him, not realizing I was staring with hatred, not lust.

I hid the piece of glass under my folded arms. My black hair covered most of my chest.

"My father told me you liked black, so I added a bit for you." He started to walk toward me. "Rose, I—"

When I heard him say my name, I lost it. I screamed and ran toward him, aiming the piece of glass at his throat.

He quickly dodged me and slammed me into the wall.

My back ached from the force. I continued to try to raise the glass to his throat. "I will never let you have me, you monster!" I spat, hatred filling my words with venom. "I know what you truly look like, you disgusting creature!"

His eyes began to glow the same rotten golden color of his father's. His true self. He grabbed my neck. "Monster?" he whispered roughly in my ear. "You won't have me, but you love the biggest monster of all, Bakusura? He has slaughtered thousands, including innocent women and children. My toll is barely in the hundreds." He smirked. "But how I do enjoy watching weak, pathetic humans die."

I struggled, but his grasp on my throat was too strong for me to fight. I glared at him.

"Maybe this will make it easier." His face began to bubble up and contort to different features. In a matter of seconds, it was done. A replica of Damien stood in front of me.

My mind knew it was false, but that didn't stop my heart from fluttering. The glass slowly slid out my hand, blood dripping to follow it.

"See? That's better," he purred as he leaned in to kiss me.

I screamed and tried to push him away, but he didn't budge. Moments before his lips touched mine, he stopped.

His grip loosened from my neck, and I felt something cold and wet on my feet. I looked down and found splatters of black blood. As I took a step back, I saw a hand, blue sparks fluttering around it, holding what looked like an organ. It oozed black blood onto the floor. I took another step back, and a man's arm came into view, pushed all the way through the prince's chest. The hand crushed the organ to a pulp, and the prince fell to his knees. The organ dropped, and the prince fell to the ground, collapsing face forward in his own black blood.

As the prince fell, I saw Damien on his knees, his arm coated in blood. Electric blue light danced around him. He had thick gashes and bite marks all over his body, and his neck was marked with three deep wounds.

I ran to him, electricity shocking me as I dropped to my knees and held him. As soon as I hugged him, I felt his body go limp. I laid him down on the floor, tears dripping down my face and onto his. He was so bruised and cut up, I barely recognized him.

"I'm sorry," he muttered through busted lips.

"Shhhh," I said as I brushed his hair from his face. I rested my head on his chest, listening to the slow beat of his heart. I began to panic. I felt like I was watching the trapped bird again. Helpless. But I'd healed the bird, hadn't I? A shot of adrenaline rushed through me. I sat up and grabbed his neck, which was losing the most blood. I focused. I wanted him healed more than anything. I willed my powers not to fail me.

I saw a tiny glitter of gold, and a sob of happiness left my throat. I kept my hands on his neck. Tinier than before, flakes drifted slowly out of my hands. The wound shrank little by little.

After about ten minutes, the flakes stopped. Damien's neck and face were mostly healed, but I couldn't heal his body. Whatever power I had in me was gone.

Damien lay asleep, his heart beating faster now.

I sighed in relief and got up. I stepped over the prince's body and took my piece of glass. They might come to check on us soon, and I couldn't risk losing Damien again. I stood over his body, not moving a muscle, watching the door intently.

After about two minutes, I heard a cough. "Rose?"

I turned around and looked down. Even slashed all over, his beauty shone through. This, I realized undoubtably was the man my heart belonged to. I kneeled down to look in his eyes. "I'm here, Damien."

He put his bloody hand on my cheek. "I couldn't lose you," he said. "I used black magic. Id forbidden myself to use it, but I don't care. You are all I care about now."

I placed my hand over his. "I love you."

He smiled. Then, as if the magnitude of the situation had suddenly struck him, he hopped up and grabbed me tight. "Rose, we have to leave now. They will do unthinkable things when they catch us."

I held back a sob. "How can we?" I said hopelessly.

He looked to the side, his eyes flicking back and forth, his brow furrowed in thought. He took the piece of mirror from my hand and carved a symbol in the carpet. Then he took a wet towel and cleaned my wounds.

"This is no time for cleaning up wounds," I said in a frantic voice.

Damien smiled, then looked at the door and softly whispered, "Bluarch alchli fuario masqureda."

An electric blue field filled the room and spread around us. I heard ferocious banging from the other side of the door and walls, and my heart started pounding.

"Only a royal Sapien's blood can call the Sapien transporters," Damien said, still cleaning my wounds.

"We're going to meet the Sapien king now? How do you plan to get a royal Sapien's blood?" I asked, frustrated. I didn't want to be in Argathia anymore.

Damien began to wring my bloody towel over the symbol on the ground. "I believe your father is the king of the Sapiens," he said.

I scoffed. "No, my father is a construction worker who lives in Jacksonville, Florida."

He looked perplexed. "Well, our lives depend on that not being true." He wrung the towel as hard as he could. Nothing.

Then a huge, hooded figure hissed to life in front of us. It looked like the figure from my room, but it was smaller, and it did not speak. It floated there as if waiting for directions.

Damien's eyes widened with shock. "Well?" he asked. "Are you going to tell him, or should I?" The crackling of his blue electricity was fading.

"Tell him what?" I demanded.

Damien brushed a piece of hair out of my face. "To take us to the Sapien king."

My real father. The veil broke, and I could hear the king's growl from the other side. "Take us to King Sapien!" I yelled as forcibly as I could.

Damien grabbed my hand, and we were swallowed in blackness.

I landed on a warm, hard, wet floor. I was soaked. I opened my eyes and realized I wasn't on the floor at all. I was on top of a drenched Damien. His arms were wrapped tightly around me. I surveyed his body, and when I made it up to his eyes, I found that he was already looking at me, analyzing my body, making sure I was okay.

My hair was drenched, and mist floated around us. But Damien's eyes made me feel warm, dry, and safe. His hair was stuck to his forehead, and water dripped down his face.

CHAPTER 9

SAPIEN KING

Without hesitation, Damien grabbed me close and kissed me slowly. It was penetrating, hard, and dominant yet soft, light, and gentle. I needed this. I needed him. We didn't get up. We barely moved. Our lips were intertwined, in a world of their own.

I heard someone clear their throat, but Damien didn't seem to care. He kept kissing me until we heard a loud hiss.

We finally separated. I looked to where the hiss was coming from.

Through the mist, I could see dozens of hooded figures as big as the one that had brought us here. They all spoke in unison. "We are the legion of Sapiens. We are here to take you to the king."

I slowly stood up, and Damien matched my movements.

The middle figure, who was the largest of the bunch, started gliding toward us. His long black robe covered his whole body, and his hood covered his face. He stopped about two feet in front of us and extended his arms, handing us two sets of hooded black robes. "Put these on," he said in a calm voice.

We put our robes over our clothes. Damien pulled his hood up so it covered his face. "It's a dishonor to the king if you show your face when you first meet him," he explained.

I pulled my hood up to cover my face and walked behind the ten hooded figures.

Damien walked beside me, making sure our arms were always touching. As the mist began to clear, two huge doors carved out of black stone appeared in front of us. They were beautiful and elegant, the black glinting with hues of green and blue. The legion of Sapiens started walking toward the door. Then, one by one, they were absorbed into it.

As the door slowly opened, I looked around. There were crystals all over the ceiling—blue, green, and purple. They gleamed brightly as the light from the door filled the dark area. It was like a cave taken over by crystals.

When the door fully opened, Damien stepped in front of me, and I followed right behind him. As we stepped through the doors, wind clung to my body, wrapping around it. It was as if I was in a windstorm, but after a second, it was gone, and I was completely dry. I looked up and saw gray stone stairs winding up to a throne. The throne was enormous and made of crystals, which pointed out jaggedly at the top and shone so brightly that my eyes dazzled. Sitting atop the throne was a hooded figure, smaller than all the others. His robe was not completely black, and silver chains encircled his waist, marked with symbols and studded with crystals.

The doors closed behind us. "Welcome," said the man in the robe. His voice was that of an old man, and he spoke very slowly. He got up and began to glide down the podium stairs. As he approached us, I realized that there wasn't a soul around us. When we'd met the other king, there had been guards everywhere, but now we were alone. "You two have caused quite a mess over in the Luthernian kingdom." His power was overwhelming and dark, but it wasn't the kind of dark that made me want to run and hide. Rather, it was a darkness that drew me in. His hooded face turned to Damien. "What an interesting turn of events." He didn't sound interested at all. His voice was emotionless. "Bakusura. Well a much weaker Bakusura."

Damien's aura began to spark, and heat started pouring off of him.

King Sapien waved his hand. "Bakusura, you do not want to battle with me. I am much older and stronger than you. I have the power to kill everything on this Earth."

I grabbed Damien's hand. It was true. He was Bakusura, one of the four originals. I'd thought the king might just have been trying to get into my head.

Damien began to calm down a little.

"I am not the same creation as when I killed you, Bakusura," King Sapien said. "We actually hold many of the same beliefs now." Sapien had been the one who had chopped Bakusura's head off.

"How could you?" I fumed. "How could you be so evil? You're just like the Luthernian king!"

The hooded figure turned slowly to face me. "I am nothing like him. Quite the contrary. We are complete opposites. He creates life, and I take it."

This was my father, I realized, and he was a cold-hearted murderer with no emotion or empathy. I ripped off my hood, tears streaming down my face, and took a step closer to him. "I am your daughter, yet you speak to me so coldly, so emotionlessly. How could my mother have ever fallen for someone like you?"

He looked at me wordlessly for a minute. Then he turned his back, and in the same monotone voice, he spoke. "My people will show you to your rooms and around my kingdom." The king disappeared behind his throne.

Two crystallized creatures walked in from the side, neither of them any taller than three feet. The smaller one was talking loudly. "I can't believe we really get to meet her!"

The other one shushed it.

As they got closer, I could see them better. They were practically transparent, sculpted out of blue and green crystals. The smaller one had a big cluster of crystals on the side of its head, and the other one's ears were pointy, jagged crystals. I could hear their feet clunking as they hit the floor.

The smaller one hurried before the bigger one. "Oh, Princess Rose! I have been waiting my whole life for this!"

The taller one rolled its crystal eyes.

The smaller of the creatures began to bow down, but its head was too heavy. The crystal cluster forced it to the ground, which it hit with a loud clunk.

The other one sighed as it helped the smaller creature up. "Pull yourself together." Its voice was nasally and hoarse.

I heard a noise from behind me and turned around to see Damien holding back a chuckle. I bent down to help the little creature back to its feet.

The little cluster-headed creature smiled at me, blue eyes twinkling.

I couldn't help but smile back.

It gave the other creature a look. "You're just mad she likes me more."

The taller creature's chest puffed out. "Good evening, Madame Rose. I am Cladiar." He bowed gracefully and pointed to the little one, sighing. "And this is Buburt."

The little one, Buburt, squeaked over him. "It is an honor to be in your presence!"

"Yes, it is," an irresistible voice said behind me.

"Ahh, Lord Bakusura" Cladiar said, bowing again. "It is an honor to meet you as well."

Buburt rolled his eyes.

"Come," Cladiar said. "Let me escort you to your room."

I grabbed Damien's hands. "Please don't leave me," I said, still feeling a little shaken.

He whispered in my ear, "Never again."

We walked through two black doors that led to a long hallway. The hallway was gray and plain, but the ceiling glittered with what looked like tiny stars. As I looked, I realized that it was a whole solar system. Planets and comets moved slowly.

"Madame Rose, your room is to the left, and Bakusura, your room is right across the hall," Cladiar announced.

Damien stopped and bent down to Cladiar.

Cladiar stumbled back, intimidated.

But Damien smiled. "It's Damien."

I could tell Cladiar wanted to question him, but he just nodded, not saying a word.

Buburt huffed. "Damien, Bakusura, doesn't matter. If you hurt the princess in any way, I'm going to climb up your spine and—"

"Buburt!" Cladiar yelled.

Damien laughed. "I appreciate your protection of the one I love, but I assure you, I will never hurt Princess Rose." He looked meaningfully into my eyes.

"All right, everyone. Move it along," Cladiar said, frustrated and pushy. "Dinner will be served in two hours."

They began to walk back down the hallway. They didn't trouble to keep their voices down.

"Buburt, you loudmouth. You always stir up trouble," Cladiar whined.

Buburt scurried behind him. "I don't trust him," he said, folding his arms.

"Oh, you jealous baboon. You just wanted her for yourself," Cladiar retorted.

Buburt began arguing, and their voices soon faded into the distance.

I turned and opened my door, Damien standing behind me. The room was blue, and it was massive. There was a small waterfall from the ceiling to the floor, the waters calm and crystal clear. There was an oversized chair made of black satin and outlined in dark-blue crystal. The floors were made of quartz and flakes of diamonds. I walked into the room and found my things from my dorm on the blue bed and the crystal desk. My eyes began to tear up, relieved to find this tiny sliver of normality.

Damien wrapped an arm around my waist, and we stood there for what seemed like hours, embracing each other. It helped settle my emotions. Finally, I turned around and gave him a kiss.

"Why don't you take a shower and get dressed," he suggested. "I'll wait for you out here."

I looked at him. "How will you get dressed and shower?"

He smiled at me. "I have my ways. Being in this castle with all this essence and energy is helping my essence heal." He pulled up his shirt and showed me where there once had been deep gashes. They were now just small red lines.

I grabbed my favorite black shirt and pants and went to take a shower. I felt warm and safe, and the overwhelming feeling of being home swept over me.

The bathroom was huge, probably the size of my house in Jacksonville. The floor was a deep blue that flickered when the light hit it. The vanity included a floor-length mirror, which was bedazzled with jade, sapphires, and diamonds. The counters were made of stones I'd never seen before, including a clear stone that was almost like diamond, only shinier. There was a white couch and a bookcase filled with books of all colors, shapes, and sizes. After looking around for a minute or two, I finally reached the shower. I was disappointed not to find a bathtub until I turned the shower on. Water trickled down from the ceiling, and it was as if I was caught in a warm rainstorm. It came out from every angle, spraying me gently. I felt so at peace, so energized and refreshed.

After my shower, I put on my shirt and jeans and went to find Damien. I didn't have to look very far. As soon as I walked out of the bathroom, there he was, standing in the middle of the waterfall, taking a shower. I blushed and looked down immediately, but it was hard to look away from the beautiful man in front of me.

His strong, broad shoulders, his big hands, and his handsome face dripped with water. Suddenly, he laughed, snapping me out of my thoughts. "You should really knock before walking in on someone taking a shower."

I turned my back to him. "That would hold true if that someone wasn't taking a shower in the middle of my room." I could still picture the water dripping down his body. My cheeks reddened. Then I felt the heat of a hand on my back.

"Are you blushing, Rose?"

I squealed. "No, I'm not!" I stuttered out, jumping away, then turning and looking at him.

He was fully clothed again, wearing a black shirt and black pants. He looked at me with fire in his eyes and grabbed my waist. "If you only knew that I feel ten times what you feel right now every time I look at you."

I swallowed thickly.

He kissed my jawline and sat down, bringing me with him. His warm embrace captivated me, and I breathed in deeply; he smelled like a fresh forest and mint. I sat next to him, and he put his arm around me. "What is that beautiful mind thinking of?" he asked.

I looked at him, taking in his beauty and dangerous aura. "You," I said. I was awestruck by him. "I want to know all about you."

He took a deep breath and lay back on the bed with his hands behind his head. "I'd much rather talk about you."

I raised an eyebrow. "Well, I asked you first."

He raised himself and leaned in so close I could taste him. "Yes, but you are so much more fascinating." He grabbed me and flung me lightly on the bed, where we began to wrestle.

I got on top of him in moments, but I knew it was because he'd let me. His strength was evident. Still, a victory was a victory. I smiled widely.

He smiled back. "How did I get so lucky? What did I do to deserve your love?" His eyes sparkled brightly, blue sparks igniting in them.

"First question," I said, still on top of him. "Why do your eyes sometimes fill with blue sparks?"

He shot me a wicked yet sexy grin and slowly started trailing his large hand up my leg.

Want and desire hit me hard, and he took it to his advantage. He whirled me around so that he was on top of me. My cheeks turned bright red.

"I'll compromise, only because I find you so irresistibly beautiful. A question for a question."

My heart was pounding, and my body filled with heat. I could barely come up with clear thoughts. I had to pull myself together. I sat up a bit.

"I normally don't compromise," Damien said ruggedly, trying to make his offer more enticing. "For you, I will, but I go first." He smiled and moved in closer, his lips brushing my ear. "Or we could wrestle some more."

My breathing grew heavy. I was so close to caving in, but he grabbed me and sat us both back up before I could.

"My eyes have blue sparks in them because electricity is always coursing through me. When I get excited or feel strong emotions, it's hard to control it. As old as I am, I've still never conquered it." He sounded disappointed in himself. He looked at me. "Now, my turn. Have you ever had a partner before … in any way?" His eyes locked on mine, curiosity taking over his face.

"No," I said shyly.

He looked relived and confused at the same time.

"Tell me about where you're from," I said.

He took a deep breath and put his hands behind his head again. “It’s beautiful, nothing like Earth or Argathia. It’s always windy, and the sun is blue and electric. I’m a royal where I’m from, one of two boys, but my parents are close-minded and arrogant, and I am nothing that they wanted me to be.” He looked off as if remembering. “They are much like Cabrakkan and his sons. They want control and war, and they will do whatever they have in order to get it.”

CHAPTER 10
THE MAN I LOVE

"I thought moving here with the three lords would solve my problems, but Cabrakkan wanted the same from me as my parents did. He wanted to build up Inner Earth and start taking over planets. Olorus finally saw the light as me, and it cost him his life. In most galaxies, it's all about conquering other people." Damien looked at me. "I have killed many people. I've done many things I am not proud of."

I put my hand on his cheek. "We all have."

He sat up straighter. "No," he argued. "Not like me," he said with regret in his voice. "I won't ever go back there. I won't be the person they wanted me to be." He looked at me, his hair covering part of his left eye. "Why do you love me? Why does such a beautiful, perfect, pure woman love a man like me?"

I stood up, frustrated. How dare he talk about himself so lowly. "I am no better than you," I said a little too loudly. "I've done things I'm not proud of, and given the circumstances, you had no choice. I probably would have done the same thing."

He stood up too, towering over me. "No," he said softly. "You would have fought. You would have died for your belief in what is right. I cowered to them. I did their dirty work. I became a war lord, killing anyone who got in my way, knowing it was wrong."

I couldn't argue with him. He was right. I would have fought to the death for what was right. I ignored his words. "I love you because you are a survivor, like me. Even when you didn't feel like you were good enough, you pushed through it. You take all my fear away, all my pain away." I laughed drily. "When you smile, it feels like home. When you touch me, I feel whole. Ever since my mom died, I've felt like a part of my soul died with her, but you have made me whole again." Tears started streaming down my face, and I made no effort to brush them away. "So, don't you dare talk about the man I love, the man who has saved me from myself, so lowly."

He held me close, and we laid down, intertwining with each other, not talking, not moving, just me on his chest, listening to his heart thump, in a place where no one could hurt us.

As we walked side by side, following Cladiar to the dining room, I couldn't help but notice all the hallway doors. One in particular stuck out to me. It was metal and black with chains that seemed to be moving slowly all around it. Something drew me to the door, almost calling me. Damien nudged me, and we continued to walk.

We entered a large empty dining room. Our footsteps echoed. The only thing in the room was a small round table and two seats carved out of rock. Beautiful carvings of two figures dancing marked the table, and blue crystals dangled from the bottom of the tabletop.

Buburt came running out with a small glass vase, which held a black rose. "I found it!" he yelled happily. He jumped on the table and placed it in the middle, breathing heavily. "A rose for Rose."

I smiled and thanked him.

Cladiar grunted. "Oh, for the love of the crystals, please go fetch dinner like you were supposed to! If Sapien finds out you took one of his roses, we'll both be in a world of trouble."

Buburt huffed. "A lady deserves flowers." He looked at Damien and scoffed.

I heard Damien chuckle, but I shot him a look to silence him. I patted Buburt on the head. "It's the most beautiful flower I have ever received," I told him.

Buburt lit up with glee.

Cladiar groaned again. "The food, Buburt."

Buburt climbed down from the table and skipped off through the back door.

"I do apologize, Madame Rose," Cladiar said. "He lets his emotions get the best of him."

I smiled. "It's okay. We all do." After a couple of moments, I realized that there were only two seats, and Cladiar was making his way toward the door. "Cladiar, why are there only two seats?"

He froze. "King Sapien will not be joining you tonight," he said stiltedly. "He is tending to other matters, but he said to give you a tour of the castle." Cladiar hurried to the back door without another word.

I turned to Damien, annoyance written all over my face. "Tending to other matters?"

Damien kissed the nape of my neck. "Would you like to tend to other matters?" He grabbed my waist and sat me down on the chair.

Damien's charm almost swept my annoyance away, but a feeling of unease still hovered over me. Cladiar and Buburt brought out a cart laden with the most delicious foods and sweets.

We ate, but I still could not shake my irritation. "I mean, does he not care that he just abandoned his daughter for eighteen years, let alone my mother?" I spat out as I took a bite of a danish. "He's the reason I'm in this mess, dragged to an unknown world." I took a sip of juice.

Damien spoke calmly. "He is also the reason you exist. He's the reason we met too, so it's hard for me to be mad at him. He brought the love of my life into my arms, even if he did chop off my head." He looked at me with such love that my heart melted, and every ounce of annoyance floated away. He then got up and hugged me from behind, wrapping his large arms around my body and chair. "I hate seeing you frustrated. Is there anything I can do?"

I sighed. He'd done so much already. "Must you be so perfect?" I got up and spun around to face him.

He gently brushed my cheek, looking at my lips. "I was thinking the same thing." He kissed me lightly.

I heard a cough from Cladiar. "I do apologize for the interruption, but Buburt and I will be heading to our quarters soon. We wondered if Madame Rose and Master Damien would like a tour of some of the castle?"

I smiled at him and nodded.

Buburt scooted his way in between Damien and me as we walked through the tall gray door to an outside area. It was nighttime, and the stars were dazzling, twinkling in the black sky, and the moon shone a bright purplish-white. There was a big green arch covered in white flowers that had an iridescent glow. I walked up ahead of the group, touching the glowing flower. It bounced and left traces of iridescent glow on my finger. The smell was warm and inviting. I had never seen such beautiful plants. As I walked beneath the arches, I was awed by the glowing flowers lighting up the garden.

Cladiar must have seen my expression. "Ahh, yes, the flowers from the king's planet. Beautiful, no?"

"Beautiful, yes," I said, walking around, taking in the fresh smell, the glowing beauty, and the relaxing feel of the garden.

Cladiar began to speak again. "They grow under the moonlight and are truly one of a kind. They even possess a little magic." I could tell Cladiar loved this garden by the way he puffed his chest out proudly.

Buburt yanked on my jeans. "This way, Rose."

I followed him down one of the narrow paths, walking by trees and bushes that swayed and sparkled brighter as we passed them. Suddenly, we stopped. Two stone chairs stood in front of a glass case. I walked in front and saw a bushel of black roses with purple flakes dancing around them. The bush was swaying left to right. It seemed that the purple flakes were feeding or preserving the roses; as soon as they started to droop, the purple flakes spruced them up again. It was magical to watch. I sat in one of the chairs, admiring the process.

Damien sat in the other chair, watching the magic in equal awe and silence.

"It's King Sapien's favorite spot," Cladiar said, interrupting the quiet. "Sometimes, he sits here for hours, never moving, just watching."

I got up reluctantly. "It is beautiful."

We walked back into the cave and passed the kitchen and other chambers, all of which featured bright, dazzling crystals. Then we started back up to our room, Buburt and Cladiar behind us. I stopped in front of the chained door again and placed my hand on it. "May we see what's inside here?" I asked.

Cladiar froze, looking as if something had stabbed him in the back. He began to stutter. "We never open that door. It is forbidden."

I looked at him with one eyebrow raised. "And why is that?"

Cladiar turned around, ignoring my question.

"Cladiar," I said lowly.

"Some things are not for me to explain, Madame Rose." He looked up at me with his crystal eyes. "If I could, I would, but please, it is nothing to fret about. Let's get you back to your room. Tomorrow will be an eventful day, and I have a special breakfast planned for you." He forced a smile.

Buburt hugged my leg and shot Damien a glare. Cladiar bowed, then walked off.

I changed into my night shorts and shirt. Damien was in my bedroom doorway, waiting on me. I jumped into the bed and told him how exhausted I was. I even fake yawned to make my lie more believable. I was going to wait for him to sleep, then go explore that door. It was calling to me. There was something there I needed to see.

Damien kissed my forehead. "I'm exhausted as well." He fell asleep with his arm around my waist.

I tried to slowly wiggle his arm loose, but it weighed down heavier. How was I going to manage this? I waited a little longer, heart pounding. I turned to face him, getting close to his body, creating a gap between his arm and my body. I tried to move his arm again, but it was as heavy as a boulder. How much did he weigh? I looked at his face. Wow, he was beautiful. His full lips and soft cheeks. He looked like an angel when he slept. "Stop ogling him. Keep it moving," I told myself.

I wiggled down, my head sliding to his chest, then to his stomach. Then, all of a sudden, he wrapped his leg around me and snored loudly. This could not be happening.

"Breathe," I said to myself. I wriggled lower and lower, sucking in as much as I could to squeeze past his leg.

Finally, I hit the floor lightly and shut my eyes. Victory was mine. I was going to find out what Sapien was hiding.

Then came a thump, and my eyes popped open. Damien's body fell on top of mine. He grabbed both of my hands and held them above my head, smiling broadly, his eyes flickering blue. "It seems I've caught a fly in my trap."

I squirmed as realization hit me. "You were awake the whole time, weren't you?"

He chuckled as he looked me up and down. "You're lucky I'm in love with you, fly." He leaned in closer to me. "Or I would eat you right up." The dangerous aura poured off him. He kissed my neck and continued to taunt me. "If you wanted to sneak off to the dungeon, you should have just asked me."

"Dungeon?" I asked.

Still atop me, he answered, "Yes. I know that spell anywhere. It's a dungeon, though I'm as curious as you are as to what Sapien has in there." He climbed off of me slowly, taking his time, savoring every feeling.

"You would really go with me?" I said.

He sighed. "As much as I enjoy watching you try to wiggle your way out of my arms, I know who you are, and there's no stopping you." He got to his feet and reached out his arm to me. "If you can't beat them, join them. It's an old war tactic."

I grabbed his hand. "How about we skip the antics next time?" I said in a huffy tone, still a little frustrated that I'd been tricked.

He purred. "But I enjoyed the antics so much." I pushed him, and he laughed, then grew serious. He looked me in the eyes. "Just so you know, Rose, I could never deny you anything. You don't need to hide anything from me. You know who I was and who I am now. I devote myself to you." He lightly kissed me and started walking.

There was no denying it. I was in love with this man. We put on our hooded coats and walked to the chained door.

Damien turned around and looked at me. "Only one condition. If you want me to open the door, when I say it's time to go, we leave."

I nodded. "Deal."

He sighed. "Also, I'm going to need a small amount of your blood for the spell."

He took a knife out of his pocket, holding my hand gently and pricking my finger. He let the blood drop on the knife, then raised my finger to his lips and kissed it. He turned to the door and started speaking in a language I didn't know. "Filopize umbrektel xineable." He smeared my blood on the door. The chains quivered and slowly slid down, and the door creaked open.

The hall was flooded with bright light, and it took a minute for our eyes to adjust. The hallway was filled with paintings, and purple and blue carpet lined the floors. Energy was vibrating throughout the space. I felt like I was floating. This was not a dungeon at all. It was a sanctuary.

Damien didn't seem to feel the same way. "This is weird," he said, looking around. "The energy in here isn't normal. I think we're on a different plain."

I giggled, high on the fumes of energy. I looked at him. "Why are you so beautiful?" I asked a little loosely.

He smiled. "Because you're getting high from the amount of energy flowing through your body."

I slapped his chest. "No, no, no!" I said, slurring my words. "You are beautiful, like a peacock's feathers." Out of the corner of my eye, I thought I saw something move. I started running its way. Was it what I was searching for?

Damien was right behind me.

I sprinted until I struck something hard. Then I looked up, and all the brightness faded away. The colorful carpets turned to gray cobblestones. There was a thirty-foot-tall wall of glass, and behind the glass stood a nine-foot-tall, winged figure resembling a dragon. Danger froze me solid, but I still wanted to touch it. I felt the creature's pain, anger, and hatred. I reached my hand out as it started to lean down toward the glass, its hand reaching for mine.

Damien yelled, "Rose, no! We need to leave now!"

But I couldn't. This creature needed me. He was hurt. Sure, he was angry, but I needed to help him, I felt somehow connected to it.

The whole place started shaking, stones falling from the ceiling.

Damien grabbed me and threw me out of the door. He slammed it shut and pressed the knife to the door, chanting quickly. He turned to me, blue static all around him, his aura black and venomous. "You promised," he said in a deep voice. "That thing was stronger and eviler than anything I have ever felt in all my life, and you tried to touch it."

I felt an ounce of guilt. "I'm sorry," I said. "It seemed so hurt."

Damien scoffed. "Hurt! The evil flowing off that thing makes Cabrakkan look like a saint!"

I was confused.

"Did you not feel it?" he asked as he helped me up from the ground.

"I mean, I felt something," I replied. "But I felt its sadness and hurt the most. It's locked up in that cage. It's probably lonely."

He huffed. "It's locked up for good reason, Rose, I assure you." He scanned my face and arms. "Are you hurt at all?"

I sighed. "I'm fine."

We walked in silence back to the room.

"I'm sorry I overreacted," Damien said. "It's just the thought of that thing touching you or hurting you …" His body started giving off static.

I grabbed his hand as we walked through the door. "I'm fine. Remember, I have thorns."

He kissed my forehead and smiled. "You are a prickly rose, aren't you?"

"Let's get some rest," I said.

I woke up to the smell of warm cinnamon. When I opened my eyes, I saw Damien sitting at the foot of my bed with a silver cart full of breakfast foods. I didn't know where I was. I was lost in happiness, but then it hit me. I probably look like a tossed pile of crap. I touched my hair. Yep, bird's nest. I touched my face. Yep, drool. I rolled my eyes and stood up to go to the bathroom, but Damien slid in front of me.

"No good morning kisses?" He leaned in and kissed my cheek, then tucked my hair behind my ears. "This morning look suits you."

I grumbled and went into the bathroom, where I brushed my hair and teeth before heading back out for a danish. I sat on the bed next to Damien. "Did Cladiar bring this?"

Damien smiled. "No, I snuck it out of the kitchen. I thought you'd enjoy breakfast in bed."

As much as I was enjoying all of these simple pleasures and the feeling of wholeness, questions raced through my mind.

Damien looked at me. "Are you okay?" he asked.

I nodded. "I just have a lot on my mind with everything going on."

"Like what?" Damien sat back and took another bite of a cinnamon breakfast bun.

"Well," I started. "Now that we're not on great terms with a powerful king who has the power to create life itself and is stronger than an ox, what's going to happen?" I thought of my friends, my father, and mine and Damien's safety. "Why hasn't he come after us? Or my friends and family?"

Damien furrowed his brow. "Rose, no matter what you choose to do, I will follow you, and I will protect you, but King Cabrakkan will stop at nothing to get what he wants. Trust me, I know you want to go back home, but the king will go after everyone you love if you go there. Your father, your friends, even people you only talked to for a second. He'll slaughter them all in front of you until you agree to his terms. It's safer if you stay here for now. I don't know what your father—"

I gave him a dirty look.

"I mean King Sapien wants to do. I'm sure they've already launched attacks, but King Sapien is very strong, and he's much older than Cabrakkan."

I sighed with discontent.

Damien put his comforting arms around me. "I'm here to the end. Whether we fight or run, I am yours."

After we finished our breakfast, we got changed and went downstairs. Cladiar and Buburt were waiting at the table with more food.

"Breakfast is served, Madame Rose." Cladiar bowed.

Buburt ran to my leg and tugged on it. "Oh, Rose, please try the white ones. They're my favorites!"

Cladiar grumbled. "Please try to have an ounce of class, Buburt."

I smiled kindly. "I'm sorry, Buburt, but I'm not hungry. I'll give them a try at lunch."

Cladiar looked past me to Damien. "I noticed there were a couple of danishes missing from my order this morning. Would you happen to know where they went?"

Damien nudged my back, and I knew he was biting back a smile behind me.

"What?" I asked in a high-pitched voice.

Damien coughed, covering up a laugh.

"Well, just so you know, breakfast should be eaten at a table with your servers." Cladiar bristled. "We are not barbarians around here."

Damien stepped in front of me. "Of course not. Do we look like barbarians?"

Cladiar looked us up and down and put his hands on his head. "Oh, for the love of the crystals, just follow me."

Buburt put his hand over his mouth and whispered, "He wasn't always this cranky and old. The cracking of his crystals really got to him."

We walked through numerous large black doors. I hadn't realized how big this cave was. Finally, I heard water rushing. We walked up to a clear door, and through it, I saw a glowing waterfall. But the water wasn't just glowing. It was blue and purple, and it glistened like diamonds. The waterfall fell into a huge swimming pool.

Cladiar interrupted my thoughts. "Your swimsuits are on the hangers to the left. There are two separate changing rooms." He eyed Damien harshly. "Please be sure to go to the correct one."

I couldn't take my eyes off the waterfall. "Cladiar, where did this come from?" I asked.

He gave a small smile. "This is from our home planet, Rose. It's much different from yours, and from Argathia, for that matter. Our planet is made up of crystals and water. This is what helps us replenish our energy. Quite frankly, it keeps us alive. So, take your time, and when you're done, press the button by the suits."

I changed into my suit, which was a dark green tankini with scale-like fabric. As I walked out of the dressing room, Damien wrapped his arms around me, kissing my neck. Together, we walked to the pool, and I slowly sank in and dunked my head under the water. This was the best feeling ever. The water connected with my skin. It was warm and silky. I felt like I was swimming in a pool of silk or floating on a cloud. I raised my head from the water and slowly felt my energy zing to life.

Damien didn't move from the top of the pool. He was watching me. "I just witnessed the most beautiful scene of my life."

I looked at him, confused.

"You," he explained. "Your energy, your movement, the way you carry yourself, the beauty that you embody. It's truly hypnotic." He jumped into the pool and was in front of me a second later. "What have you done to me, Rose?"

I smiled. Everything he felt, I felt too. He was the most irresistible man I had ever met. His aura, his smile, his energy. I couldn't get enough of him. We swam and talked for hours. I felt energized, so on top of the world.

Eventually, Damien looked at me, astounded. "Rose, you're glowing."

I smiled. "Thank you."

He grabbed my hand and pulled it in front of my face. "No, you're literally glowing."

Sure enough, there was an iridescent glow all around me. "That's so weird," I said, looking down at myself.

"It's just like those glowing flowers in the garden," Damien said, analyzing me. He clenched his jaw. "Rose, when you healed me that day, did the king touch you?"

I looked down and winced a little. "He threw me at the wall and broke my ribs. Then he healed me with his magic."

The water suddenly became very hot and started bubbling. Damien's eyes were completely blue, and his aura was black, making my heart thump hard. "Why didn't you tell me earlier? I would have gone back and ripped him limb from limb."

I grabbed Damien. "The king can create armies," I said. "He can make people freeze in place. You have to promise me you'll never go back there."

Damien rose up, and even though he was only six foot four, he seemed to tower at least eight feet over me. "Do you think I can't kill that infidel now that I know his tricks? I mapped out his whole kingdom, all his sons' rooms. He will never catch me off-guard again. I'm going to murder his entire lineage." His voice growled, and sparks zoomed around him, his eyes shining a white blue.

I realized I was no longer talking to Damien. I was talking to Bakusura, the war lord, the leader. I got up and threw my arms around him. His energy stunned me, and I was terrified, but love spurred me on. "This is not who you are anymore, Damien," I whispered. "We survived him, and we will take care of him the right way. We'll hold a trial. We'll make him pay for his crimes. But not like that. Feel me." I pressed myself against him, burying my head in his chest.

Damien slowly started to calm down and turn back into himself. The blue sparks started to slow, and he sank into my arms. "Forgive me," he said in a voice full of shame.

"Always," I whispered in his ear as I rubbed his head.

"I should have been there to protect you."

I shushed him, and we cuddled there until Cladiar came to the pool to tell us that it was time for dinner.

CHAPTER 11

MY FATHER

"I was going to murder him, you know," Damien said.

I looked up at him, watching water drip down his perfect nose.

"When I saw the son of Cabrakkan coming through that door, all my anger rose up. He killed my best friend right before my eyes. He treated all the women like garbage just like his father did. He deserves worse than death. I was giving him mercy, I told myself." He sighed. "But then I looked at you, and I knew you deserved better than a murderer." He smiled gently. "You deserve better than me. But I am going to try my best to be the man you deserve. I promise. I will only kill when protecting those I love." He kissed me on the forehead and began to get up. "We'd better go before Cladiar sends the calvary after us if we're late for dinner."

As I got up, I noticed my foot was still glowing a little. "Why did you ask if the king had healed me?" I asked.

He was out of the pool already. He reached for my hand. "I have a theory," he told me. "I believe that any magic that you touch, you retain as your own for a certain period of time."

I was intrigued. I looked at him expectantly, urging him to continue.

"Most royal blood has some type of power. Whether it's used for good or bad is up to the person," Damien explained. Then he smiled. "It's just a theory, though."

I looked at him. "What are your powers?" I asked. "I mean, is there more than one?"

He helped me up. "Usually, there is only one power, but some people can use black and light magic. We must use blood to unlock it or activate it." He sighed. "As you already know, I have electricity running through my body. It also gives me very fast speed."

I interrupted. "The speed of light!"

He laughed. "At times, but it takes a lot of energy to run that fast."

"Is that how you got to me?" I asked.

He nodded, then wrapped his arms around me. "Would you like to see a little?"

I smiled excitedly. "Cladiar will be furious," I said.

He smiled devilishly. “He’ll have to catch us first.”

He took me in his arms, and I grabbed onto his neck. It felt like gravity slowed, and everything was in slow motion. The waterfall barely seemed to be flowing as we ran past it. It looked as though he was walking on water. Blue lines sped all around us. I felt the wind in my hair, and I closed my eyes. It was as if I was flying. I felt weightless. I let out a laugh.

We came to an abrupt halt as an angry Cladiar appeared in front of us, tapping his foot. “Why do I even bother with you two? Really, it’s like whatever I say goes in one ear and out the other.”

“I think he caught us,” I whispered in Damien’s ear.

He tried to hold back a smile.

“Proper education is a joke in Outer Earth, I take it,” Cladiar fumed. “Well, thank the crystals I’m not from that awful place.” He squinted at us. “Please dress yourselves and try to hurry.”

We got dressed and went to dinner, whispering and smiling. Our dinner was waiting for us, and Buburt was very excited to see us. But there were still only two chairs.

I looked at Cladiar. “Only two chairs.”

Cladiar’s expression changed quickly. “Yes. King Sapien sends his best regards. He could not make it tonight.”

Heat started in my toes and rose to my chest. “He can’t make it tonight or won’t make it?”

Cladiar dropped his head.

"I'm fine with this charade," I said. "If he won't come to me, I'll go to him and tell him where he can put the regards he sends."

"Please, Madame Rose. Don't."

"Cladiar, don't test me," I said. "Just tell me where he is. I'm done with this."

Cladiar puffed out his chest. "I cannot," he said, holding his head high. "I will follow my king's request."

"Your king is a coward!" I yelled.

He looked taken aback.

"Miss Rose, please don't yell. I don't like to see you upset," Buburt said sadly.

Cladiar gritted his teeth. "Don't you dare, Buburt," he said warningly.

Buburt blurted out, "He's in his chambers at the top of the castle, behind the green door!" "BUBURT!" Cladiar yelled.

I didn't hear the rest because I ran. I ran as fast as I could up the stairs, tears welling up in my eyes. I was tired of this. My own father had been ignoring me my whole life, and even now that I was here, he wouldn't talk to me. With each step I took, I became more enraged. Between the running upstairs and the anger swelling in my chest, it was growing hard to breathe. Finally, I reached the green door. I flung it open and stared angrily into the room.

There he was. The hooded figure too cowardly to show himself, too cowardly to talk to his daughter. He stood in front what appeared to be a large crystal computer. His old voice crackled to life. "Didn't Cladiar tell you I was busy?"

I scoffed. "You are a coward, a selfish, egotistical coward." I laced my words with venom, hoping to hurt him, hoping to get some kind of reaction from this cold, emotionless being.

He slowly turned to me. "If you came here to fight, I'm afraid you will be disappointed."

I stormed over to him, looking up at the blackness that hid his face. "I came here to tell you that you are a disappointment as a father. You are a cowardly being who didn't deserve my mother's love." Tears welled up in my eyes, but I blinked them back. "You never cared about us. You should have just left her alone. Look at this mess I'm in!" I yelled, tears now falling down my face.

He stood motionless. "Perhaps you are right."

My heart felt like a dagger had pierced through it. He truly didn't care. He was incapable of caring.

"But one must know the whole truth before forming opinions," he continued. He reached out a long finger. "May I?"

I didn't know what he wanted. I didn't know what to say.

"I can show you the answers you seek," he told me.

That was all I needed to hear. I nodded, and he placed his palm over my head, chanting loudly.

Wind danced around my face, and heat filled my head as my eyes rolled back. I was him. I was in his body, watching me with my eyes closed and his hand atop my head. Then, in a flash, I was in his memories.

We were in a beautiful place filled with crystals. He—or was it me? —was watching his father, a bulky man with scaly skin and a huge horn on his head, talk down to his mother. She was beautiful, small, and fragile with skin like ice and long white hair. He felt angry, but he couldn't express his emotions. That night, he woke up and ran to his mother. She was crying and had bruises on her face. She told him to leave, but he didn't. He just stood there, wide-eyed. He wanted to hug her, but he didn't. Why didn't he? That night, he pledged to take his mother and leave that awful place for somewhere safe.

The next day, he was outside. The sky was bright orange. He squinted his eyes, looking up. He saw an animal that resembled a cat but had six tails and was a yellowish color with beady black eyes. It was crying in pain. Its leg was caught in a trap, and it was bleeding out. He ran to it, and it flinched in fear. He tried to take the trap off, but it was locked on. As the creature screamed, he felt sadness, hurt, and compassion. He kneeled down and grabbed the animal in his arms. Something jolted through him, and the animal calmed. It looked up at him thankfully. Then it curled into his chest and died. He grew angry. "Why?" he yelled. "Why couldn't I have a different power? This is a curse!" He dug a hole with his hands and buried the animal. He then heard his mother scream.

He ran up the crystal steps and saw his father throwing his mother around again. "I said I wanted you back in ten minutes, not fifteen." He hit her in the face, and blood splattered all over the clear crystal. His dad laughed as she curled up beneath him.

"Stop," Sapien whispered.

His dad looked at him, enraged. "Don't test me, Sapien." He kicked Sapien's mother in the stomach.

Sapien's eyes went black with rage. He ran to his father and plunged both his hands into his stomach. His father started jolting in pain, blood coming out of his eyes and mouth. He made a loud thud as his body hit the floor.

It was only then that Sapien heard his mother screaming. "No!"

He turned to her, confused.

"Why did you do that?" she shouted at him. "You fool!" She pushed Sapien out the way and ran to lie down beside his father. "Leave!" she screamed. "Leave, and don't ever come back. You are no son of mine."

At that moment, something happened to Sapien. The emotions he'd had shriveled and died, and he felt nothing.

Another memory flashed by. He was here, in Argathia, talking with Lord Cabrakkan.

"Olorus is planning an attack on our people," Cabrakkan said.

Sapien bristled. He didn't like Cabrakkan, but he didn't want a war either.

"I know we all agreed to live in peace," Cabrakkan continued. "But Olorus doesn't just want to migrate humans down here. He also wants all of Inner Earth for himself."

Sapien didn't like that. This was his safe place to get away from all the other worlds. He did a spell to check if Cabrakkan was lying. He was not.

We flashed to another memory. Cabrakkan's creations were yelling, and the world was filled with fire and swords and rioters by their thousands. Sapien and Cabrakkan spoke a foreign language and opened the door. Olorus sat there, drinking with another man—a man with honey-brown eyes that began to spark blue when he saw them enter. Damien. My Damien.

They tied Olorus up. Sapien grabbed Damien.

Damien's life started to slip. "You have been fooled, Sapien, old man, and you will get what you deserve," he whispered.

Sapien saw Bakusura's spirit leave to another body. He said nothing.

Cabrakkan laughed.

"We wanted peace!" Olorus yelled.

Cabrakkan's eyes flared golden-red. He roared, "You will find peace in death!" He then chopped Olorus's head off and started cheering with the crowd. "Find all the humans! Kill them all!" he shouted.

Suddenly, everyone heard a woman scream. She was surrounded by black. Her energy was powerful and unforgiving. "You will all regret the day you murdered my love, who stood for justice and truth!" She took a knife and slit her wrist. "Reap your pain!" she hollered. She then started chanting in an unrecognizable language. She was pulsating.

Sapien looked through the door and saw the moon trembling. He smelled death.

All the women started dropping to the ground, dead. The men scattered, some trying to leave the planet. Then the moon turned blood-red, and the men started dying as well.

"Stop running, fools. This is just a trick," Cabrakkan ordered. But he started to realize that it was so much more than that.

Sapien looked at Olorus's dead body and saw his daughter curled over it, crying in rage. Her white hair slowly turned black.

Cabrakkan grabbed her by her hair. "You will marry me, and you will breed my heirs."

She punched him in the face. "Over my dead body."

Sapien liked her spirit. He'd never seen a woman fight back before.

Her eyes changed from blue to green. Cabrakkan was about to slap her when Sapien took her under his coat and spoke a spell to zip them safely to his cave. They fell to a halt in the very room we were in now.

"You monster!" she screamed.

I realized as she got up that this woman was my mother. My heart skipped a beat, and so did Sapien's.

"You're welcome," he said.

"Welcome?" she scoffed. "You murdered my father, you filth!"

He sighed. "Actually, Cabrakkan murdered your father. I murdered Bakusura."

That made her even more angry. "I'm going to kill you!" She lunged toward him, screaming.

He dodged her. "Stop it before you kill yourself."

But she didn't stop. She chased him around the room, screaming and yelling at the top of her lungs.

This went on for hours until she finally ran out of energy. Her breathing slowed down. Quietly, she again vowed, "I'm going to kill you."

Sapien was frustrated. "I am already dead," he said in a monotone voice. But there was something else there. Passion? Anger? "I'm dead inside and out. If you touch my hands, you will die too."

My mother looked at him, confused and livid.

He turned away, not able to bear looking at her as he told her the truth. "I was fooled," he said shamefully. "I thought Olorus wanted war and—"

She cut him off. "My father would never!"

"I know that now!" Sapien yelled back. Then he coughed and regained himself. "I know that now," he repeated. "Cabrakkan came to me and said that Olorus wanted war."

My mother scoffed. "And you just believed him?"

"No," Sapien told her. "I did a foolproof spell on him. If he was lying, it would have told me."

She scowled. "Cabrakkan's family dates back from the times when black magic was first created. He would have been prepared for your spell."

Sapien fell silent, amazed by her knowledge and wit.

"Well, two innocent men are dead because your parlor trick didn't work," my mother continued. She stepped closer to him. "You owe your life to them."

He looked at her, and he realized that she was breathtaking, perfect in every way. Her energy and spirit made him feel something where there was usually nothing.

"Take it, then," he told her. He put his arms up. "There's a knife in that drawer. Cut my head off, and I will die. You are right. Innocent blood is on my hands."

She ran to the drawer and pulled out the long blade.

He truly didn't care. He didn't want to live anyway.

My mother put the blade up to his neck and pressed it into his skin, watching his eyes, which never left her. But she couldn't do it. "You are despicable!" she yelled.

He reeled back. "I am letting you kill me," he argued.

She huffed. "Well, now that you've told me everything you have, how can I? I would be no better than you." She threw her hands up.

"I am truly sorry," he said, meaning every word.

She gave him a side glance. "Yes, you are."

We flashed to yet another memory. I didn't know how much time had passed. Sapien was walking through the big arch, but instead of a beautiful garden, there was nothing but cobblestone and a couple of crystals. Sapien sat on one of the crystals, looking up at the sky. He heard a voice that made his heart flutter.

"You know this place is a pile of rocks, literally," my mother said in a snarky tone.

"Well, maybe that's how I like it," Sapien replied.

She smiled slightly. "Not even a dead man would like this place." She walked past him. "If I'm going to be stuck here for the time being, I might as well spruce it up a bit."

Sapien felt a jolt of happiness. "You're choosing to stay here?"

"For the time being," she said shortly. "This would make a beautiful garden. Why don't you plant some flowers?"

Sapien sighed. "Because everything I touch dies," he said in a cold voice.

"Oh, really?" she asked, raising an eyebrow and walking toward him.

"What are you trying to do?" he asked, feeling nervous and excited.

She took a step forward. "Give me your hand," she said.

"No." He stepped back.

She repeated, "Give me your hand."

"You will die!" he yelled at her in a voice he didn't recognize.

She changed her demeanor. "Give me your hand, please."

"I will do no such thing."

My mother huffed. "Fine," she said. She turned around, then quickly turned back and grabbed his hand swiftly.

"No!" he screamed. But it was too late. His hand was touching hers. His heart started racing. But nothing happened. He looked up at her.

She closed her eyes. Purple flakes began to dance around their hands. "You see, you might have the power of death," she explained, "but my power is the opposite of whatever power touches me."

He looked deep into her eyes and realized that he was completely in love.

We flashed to another memory. Sapien was in the garden again, but this time, it was full of the beautiful flowers I'd seen before. There was one empty space left.

Sapien watched my mother, his heart so full of love and happiness that it was almost overwhelming. She was sweating, dirt all over her face and her hair messy, but he thought she was the most beautiful thing in the world.

"All right," she said. "You're planting the last one." She handed him a rosebush in a pot. "All you have to do is dig a hole and plant it."

"They're going to die, Alana," Sapien said matter-of-factly.

"You don't know until you try, Sapien," she countered. "Let's do it."

He would do anything to make her happy, even planting a plant he knew was going to die right away. He dug the hole and picked up the plant. Slowly but surely, the petals began to turn black.

But as they started to die, my mother came in and touched the plant with him. The plant began to change. Purple flakes danced around the roses, and even though they stayed black, they also stayed alive.

Sapien looked at her lovingly, and they kissed.

We fast-forwarded to one last memory. Sapien was drenched in sweat, a sword in his hand and fifty bodies before him.

My mother came out with a round belly, tears running down her cheeks. "We can't live like this anymore, Sapien. He will never stop coming for me. I'm the last true-blooded royal woman of my race."

"Alana, my love," Sapien said. "I will never let him touch you."

She looked at him with love in her eyes. "He knows more magic than us, and his soul is cold and black," she croaked. "He will kill our child."

Sapien hissed. "Never!" he roared, feeling pain in his heart.

"He will keep creating armies, darling," my mother said. "I can no longer put you and our child in danger. I love you today, tomorrow, and forever." She kissed him.

He was so confused that he couldn't move. Then everything went black.

I snapped back into my body.

Sapien started talking, his voice emotionless once more. "She left a letter for my eyes only. She begged me never to come looking for her, and she hid her essence from everyone in the universe. I searched for you and her. I couldn't leave Argathia, and she knew that, but I sent my spirits. I could never find a trace of either of you. I mourned for years until I grew cold inside again and felt nothing. When I saw you arrive, you looked just like her. Cabrakkan has already attacked many times, and he will send armies again. It is hard for me to express myself, and right now, I need to focus on protecting you and protecting our home. I cannot let what happened to your mother happen to you too."

My heart sank. My father didn't hate me or my mother. He loved my mother, and he wanted to protect me.

"I am so happy I found love with your mother and that you grew up to be just like her," Sapien told me. "If I die today, I will die happy." He paused. "I love you, Rose. Don't ever change who you are, it's your destiny to change this world. I wish we could spend more time together."

Damien came rushing through the door, moving as fast as he could. "Run" he screamed at me in desperation and anger.

Before any of us could move, an overpowering energy launched into the room. Something fell from the roof, breaking it to pieces right behind Sapien.

"Run!" I screamed at Sapien as the big black figure stood behind him.

He didn't move. It was as if he knew the end was inevitable even if he did. He looked at Damien. "Protect my Rose," he said.

A huge creature with horns and wings grabbed the top of Sapien's head, then roared a roar that made my knees go weak. The creature took a sword and chopped my father's head off. My father's body dropped to the floor with a thud, and the creature rolled his head to my feet and Sapiens blood splattered over my legs and stomach.

I was paralyzed by fear. His energy was overwhelming, making it hard to breathe. Tears stung my eyes. As I stood with tears running down my face and blood splattered all over my body, I couldn't help but turn to him. As he ran toward me, his hair stuck to his face and his eyes flaring blue with determination, he shouted at me to run. His face filled with passion and anger, and his aura screamed with protection.

Everything in my head slowed down. I couldn't have moved even if I'd wanted to. The more I stood in place, the angrier he became. He knew that if I stayed, I would die. But the truth was, I wouldn't want to die anywhere else but here, by his side. Forgetting the world, the pain, the lies, and the cards I'd been dealt, I smiled at him.

He roared in anger. He knew I wasn't leaving. He knew I was preparing for my death.

The face of evil began to walk toward me, dragging the blood-stained sword on the ground.

As he became closer, he started transforming from a huge dragon-like beast to a tall man with the same features as me, the same green eyes and black hair. "Hello, sister," he said maliciously smiling.

Printed in Great Britain
by Amazon